"Statistically speaking, this is kind of alarming," Marshall said. "Two dead women, each of whom happens to share a name with one of your past aliases, both turning up dead in the past few weeks? I don't like the sound of this."

Tell me about it, Sydney thought. A disturbing picture was definitely forming. "What's the next name on the list?"

Marshall worked through the list with dismaying ease. Less than an hour later, an unmistakable pattern had emerged:

Molly Zerdin, thirty-one. Found hanging from a lamppost on the Venice boardwalk. Sydney had posed as a Molly Zerdin six years before, on assignment in Oxford, England.

Christina Auriti, thirty. Found stuffed into a trash bin on Rodeo Drive. Not to be confused with Christina Auriti of Auriti Antiquities, Sydney's cover in Mexico City during the Rambaldi clock affair.

Four women dead, Sydney counted. *In less than a month.* She felt sick to her stomach. There was no way to deny the awful truth.

Someone is killing my namesakes.

Also available from
SIMON SPOTLIGHT ENTERTAINMENT

ALIAS™

THE
apo™
SERIES

ALIAS™

THE

SERIES

NAMESAKES

BY GREG COX

An original novel based on the
hit TV series created by J. J. Abrams

SSE

SIMON SPOTLIGHT ENTERTAINMENT
New York   London   Toronto   Sydney

This book is a work of fiction. Any references to historical events, real people, or real locales are used fictitiously. Other names, characters, places, and incidents are the product of the author's imagination, and any resemblance to actual events or locales or persons, living or dead, is entirely coincidental.

SSE

SIMON SPOTLIGHT ENTERTAINMENT
An imprint of Simon & Schuster
1230 Avenue of the Americas, New York, New York 10020
Text and cover art copyright © 2006 by Touchstone Television.
All rights reserved, including the right of reproduction in whole or in part in any form.
SIMON SPOTLIGHT ENTERTAINMENT and related logo are trademarks of Simon & Schuster, Inc.
Manufactured in the United States of America
First Edition 10 9 8 7 6 5 4 3 2 1
Library of Congress Control Number 2006923100
ISBN-13: 978-1-4169-2442-5
ISBN-10: 1-4169-2442-6

ALIAS™

To: Authorized Personnel Only
From: Archives (Classified)
Re: Mission Chronology

Note: The events described in this dossier take place shortly before APO Mission 4.20, code-named "The Descent."

LA BREA TAR PITS
LOS ANGELES

A family of prehistoric mammoths posed around the edges of the bubbling tar pit. The life-size replicas drew wide-eyed stares from the throng of fourth graders visiting the site. Digital cameras whirred busily as the children chattered among themselves. A sunny blue sky provided ideal weather for their field trip.

"Welcome to Rancho La Brea," Dan Tillworth said, greeting the students and their hassled teacher. The volunteer tour guide raised his voice to be heard over the babble of childish voices, not to mention the traffic on nearby Wilshire Boulevard. "Thanks for showing up here so bright and early this morning. Are you ready to learn about the pits?"

A chorus of enthusiastic voices answered in the affirmative.

"Great!" Dan said sincerely. He was anxious to get the tour started. The fourth graders from Buena Vista Elementary were the first group tour of the morning, but they were hardly the only field trip expected that day. He had a long shift ahead of him. "Let's get going!"

Ferns surrounded what looked like a large, greasy pond in the southeast corner of Hancock Park. Bubbles broke the oily surface of the pool as pockets of methane and hydrogen sulfide accompanied the gummy black asphalt seeping up from beneath the water. A smell like rotten eggs made the children wrinkle their noses. "Whoa, that stinks!" one of the kids exclaimed.

Dan led the group over to the wire fence guarding the perimeter of the pit. With his back to the bubbling ooze, he launched into his spiel. "The La Brea Tar Pits are one of the world's most famous repositories of prehistoric fossils. During the last ice age roughly ten thousand to forty thousand years ago, mammoths, saber-tooth tigers, and other now-extinct animals and plants were trapped in the sticky asphalt and preserved forever. Even today many small birds and insects are snared in the tar every year."

"Like that lady?" one kid asked.

Lady? Dan glanced over at the child, who was pressing his face against the wire fence. A horrified gasp escaped the guide's lips as he spotted what the boy was looking at.

Lying along the shore of the pond, half-submerged beneath the muck, was the body of a young woman, obviously quite deceased. Glassy eyes stared blankly back at Dan and the kids. Gooey pitch was smeared over the corpse's face and upper body. Streaks of asphalt clung to the woman's pink velour jogging suit. Although the woman's features were obscured by the goo, she looked to have been in her mid-thirties. Dan didn't think he had ever seen her before.

"Oh my God . . ."

The other children rushed forward to see, even as their teacher struggled to herd them away from the grisly sight. A few of the more sensitive kids started crying. The teacher's face looked just as pale as Dan imagined his own countenance must be. A little boy vomited onto the walkway. Dan knew exactly how he felt.

"That's it!" he blurted out. "The tour is over!"

According to the report the police filed, the woman's driver's license identified her as Christiana Stephens.

The name meant nothing to Dan.

CHAPTER 1

EDGEWOOD GARDENS, PENNSYLVANIA
ONE MONTH EARLIER

Originally the private arboretum of a wealthy nine-teenth-century philanthropist, Edgewood Gardens was now open to the general public. More than one thousand acres of sprawling gardens, woodlands, and meadows attracted scores of nature-loving tourists from all over the world who ambled along Edgewood's shady walkways as they took in the intoxicating sights and scents of the gardens' lavish horticultural displays. A gentle breeze wafted through the warm April air. Birds chirped in the tree-tops. A squirrel ran up the trunk of a leafy oak tree.

There are worse places to be on assignment, Sydney Bristow thought. She breathed in the rich floral aroma of the native azaleas. Daffodils, magnolias, and purple hyacinths blossomed in a gentle hollow alongside the path. An elegant glass conservatory rose in the distance. *This beats an industrial park in Siberia any day.*

The undercover agent strolled down a paved walkway, seemingly intent on enjoying the sylvan serenity all around her. She was dressed casually, in a tank top, shorts, and stylish sneakers. A baseball cap protected her face from the glare from the abundant sunshine and helped conceal her features. A pair of tinted sunglasses added to her disguise. An innocuous-looking brown handbag was strapped over her shoulder, and her oversize star-shaped silver stud earrings glinted in the sunlight. A light brown ponytail bounced against the back of her neck.

Her relaxed body language was deceptive. Behind her shades, Sydney's eyes were focused on a short, middle-aged Asian woman walking several feet in front of her. Dr. Yvonne Wong had made an effort to hide her own identity, sporting a wide-brimmed hat and dark glasses, but it was to no avail; Sydney had been trailing Wong ever since the CIA-employed chemist had first set foot in the gardens.

According to Hayden Chase, director of the Central Intelligence Agency, the CIA had reason to believe that Wong was being blackmailed to supply classified tech secrets to an unknown party. Worried that Wong might have accomplices within the agency, and anxious to keep knowledge of the possible security leak under wraps, Chase had tasked APO to quietly look into the matter. Since APO didn't officially exist, the top-secret black-ops unit was ideal for this sort of clandestine investigation . . . which is why Sydney found herself shadowing Wong on this warm and sunny afternoon.

Certainly, the scientist in question was acting guilty as hell. Unlike Sydney, she kept glancing around nervously, as though afraid of being recognized, and she walked hurriedly down the path, paying little or no attention to the brightly blooming flowers along the way. *You can tell she's no field agent,* Sydney thought. The other woman looked like she was going to jump out of her skin at any moment. *I couldn't behave that suspiciously if I tried.*

Sydney wondered what the blackmailer had on Wong. So far, APO's preliminary research hadn't turned up any of the usual smoking guns: financial problems, drug habits, gambling debts, illicit love affairs, et cetera. Wong's background was squeaky clean, with no indication that she was any sort of double agent or mole. She had no husband to cheat on, no children to threaten or hold hostage. As of this morning, her parents were still living peacefully in a retirement home outside Baltimore. Her personal politics were boringly middle of the road; she hadn't even voted in the last election. Ideology was not a factor; the most subversive organization she belonged to was the American Chemical Society.

With any luck, we should have the answer soon, Sydney mused. Prior surveillance indicated that Wong was on her way to rendezvous with her blackmailer. Ideally, Sydney and her fellow agents hoped to catch both Wong and the unknown extortionist in the act. Hayden Chase and APO were determined to find out who had turned Wong in the first place—and what they wanted with the stolen technology. *That's the big fish,* Sydney reminded herself. *Wong is just the bait.*

Wong glanced back over her shoulder, and Sydney pretended to be captivated by a bed of pink and white lilacs. Sydney lingered by the flowers, letting a family of Belgian tourists come between her and the other woman. She wasn't worried about letting Wong get a little farther ahead of her. If their intel was correct, she knew exactly where the nervous chemist was heading.

Hurry up, Yvonne, she silently urged Wong. *You don't want to keep your blackmailer waiting.*

The scientist's gaze moved past Sydney without stopping. Even though both women had worked for the CIA at various points in their careers, they had never met before, so Sydney was not surprised that Wong did not recognize her. Plus, Sydney was based out of Los Angeles, while Wong worked at Langley. These days, of course, Sydney was even more anonymous. Only Chase and a few others knew she was still on the Agency's payroll.

Apparently satisfied that no one was following her, Wong continued down the path toward the center of the gardens. Sydney waited a couple of seconds, then strolled after her target at a leisurely pace. Within minutes they approached an open courtyard dominated by an elegant marble fountain.

White water erupted into the air before cascading down into a tiled stone basin. Beyond the fountain was a hedge maze composed of closely packed yews. Evergreen walls that stood more than seven feet high guarded the shadowy entrance to the maze.

Almost there, Sydney thought. "Phoenix to Outrigger," she whispered into a concealed miniature communicator. "We're heading your way."

"Copy that, Phoenix," a familiar voice replied in her ear. She recognized the deep bass tones of her partner, Marcus Dixon. "I have the target in sight."

Sydney spotted Dixon on the opposite side of the courtyard, a distinguished-looking black man, some nineteen years older than she, disguised as one of Edgewood's small army of gardeners. He watered the outer walls of the maze with a garden hose while covertly monitoring the situation. Dixon and Sydney had gone through a lot together; she knew she could count on him to watch her back, no matter what.

"Any sign of Wong's contact?" she asked him.

"Negative." Dixon kept his gaze fixed on the thirsty hedges. "If the blackmailer is here, he's not making himself known yet."

Too bad, Sydney thought. Spray from the fountain blew against her face as she surveyed the scene. The warm weather had brought out a good-size crowd; dozens of visitors passed through the courtyard as they explored the gardens. A preppy couple walked hand in hand. An overweight retiree cruised along in an electric scooter. Smiling parents pushed a stroller. Wong could be here to meet any one of them.

Carved stone benches offered relief to weary feet, but Wong was too keyed up to take advantage of them. Instead, she paced restlessly in front of the maze, peering frequently at her wristwatch. Like Sydney, she searched the faces of the crowd, but in a far more obvious fashion. A four-year-old would have known that Wong was waiting for someone. For the CIA's sake, Sydney hoped that Wong was a better scientist than she was a spy. Even Marshall looked cooler in the field.

Wong checked her watch again. Sydney began to worry that the petite chemist had been stood up. Had Wong's agitated manner scared off her blackmailer? She wondered how long the jittery scientist would wait for her rendezvous. Wong looked ready to bolt at any moment.

Hang on, Yvonne, Sydney thought. There was no point in nabbing Wong alone. Even if they caught her with classified material on her person, that wouldn't bring them any closer to the mastermind behind the blackmail plot. If necessary, Sydney was willing to wait all day to find out who was in the market for stolen CIA tech secrets. But could Wong's nerves hold out that long?

"You think we've been made?" she asked Dixon. Faking a yawn, she placed a hand over her mouth to conceal her moving lips. "What if someone spotted me following her?"

"Unlikely," he answered. "You're too good for that."

Sydney appreciated the vote of confidence, but it didn't make waiting any easier. Minutes dragged on interminably as she wandered idly about the courtyard. Then, just when she was convinced that the blackmailer was going to be a no-show, a well-groomed couple emerged from the hedge maze and approached Wong. Sydney's heart sped up. This could be it!

Making a point not to look directly at the encounter, she fished a compact camera from her handbag and feigned an interest in the fountain. In fact, the camera had been ingeniously designed (by Marshall Flinkman, op-tech inventor extraordinaire) to observe subjects at a right angle to the direction in which it appeared to be pointed. Thus, Sydney was able to zoom in on the new arrivals as she seemed to be focusing on the fountain. She clicked away, capturing the strangers' faces for future reference. A built-in parabolic microphone allowed her to eavesdrop on the encounter from several feet away.

"Excuse me," one of the newcomers said, addressing Wong. He was a stocky man wearing a neatly pressed white suit. Sydney thought his creepy features looked vaguely familiar, but she couldn't place him right away. His eyes were a freakish yellow hue and he had slicked-back black hair that had gone gray at the temples. Bushy black eyebrows met above his puglike nose, and a thick handlebar mustache drooped past both sides of his mouth, framing a lantern jaw. His voice held a distinct German accent. "Do you know if the lilies are in bloom?"

"Only the v-violet ones," Wong stammered nervously. "In the conservatory."

The German nodded approvingly; obviously,

Wong had provided the correct response. His companion, a statuesque blonde, stood silently at his side, holding on to his hand. Her flaxen tresses, which were piled up in a bun, crowned her smooth white brow, and a cotton halter top and tight white slacks showed off an Amazonian physique worthy of a female bodybuilder. Her striking blue eyes coolly scanned the courtyard while her exquisite cheekbones looked like they could cut through glass. A bulge beneath one of her polished leather boots hinted at the presence of a concealed weapon.

The German's bodyguard? Sydney speculated. She took note of the couple's clasped hands. *Or perhaps something more?*

"A pleasure to meet you, Dr. Wong," the man said. Now that the scientist had given the proper response, the German was ready to do business. "Forgive the delay. My colleague and I had to make certain that you had truly come alone, as instructed."

Sydney was glad to hear that she and Dixon had apparently escaped the couple's surveillance. *Let's hear it for that expert SD-6 training.*

"I did everything you asked, I promise!" Wong insisted. The parabolic microphone picked up the nervous tremor in her voice. "I just want this whole nightmare to be over with."

"First things first," the German said. "Do you have the formula?"

Formula for what? Sydney wondered. The exact nature of the information sought by the blackmailer remained unclear. Regardless, she had no intention of letting the German or his imposing colleague exit the gardens with their prize.

"Yes," Wong answered. She looked around furtively before retrieving a computer disk from her purse. The German reached for the disk, but Wong hesitated before letting go of it. Guilt was written all over the woman's face. "I can't believe I'm doing this. . . ."

"Then perhaps you should not have fled the scene of that accident," the German accused her. His suave voice held little sympathy as he snatched the disk from her fingers. "I must say, the phrase 'hit-and-run' sounds particularly ugly in English."

"It wasn't my fault!" Wong blurted out. "That boy came out of nowhere! I tried to stop the car, but it all happened so quickly!" She wrung her hands, barely able to contain herself. "Please, you can't show anyone those photos!"

So that's *what the blackmailer has on Wong,* Sydney realized. She couldn't help wondering whether the German or his associates had staged the accident in the first place, to set up Wong in a compromised position. *Probably,* she decided. *Lord knows enemy agents have gone to even more elaborate lengths to get hold of classified information.*

The German tucked the disk into the inside of his jacket. "Once we have verified that the formula is genuine, the incriminating footage will be destroyed. In the meantime, our business here is concluded. Thank you for your cooperation, doctor."

That's my cue, Sydney thought. Putting away her camera, she began to close in on Wong and the nameless couple. Still watering the hedges, Dixon inched toward the trio as well. Sydney scowled as she contemplated the swarms of innocent bystanders populating the area. Apprehending Wong and the others was going to be tricky; the last thing she wanted was for civilians to be caught in a crossfire.

Her gaze darted to the suspicious bulge in the Amazon's boot. "The blonde appears to be armed," she warned Dixon via the comms. "I'm going to take her out first."

"Copy that, Phoenix. Good luck."

Sydney crossed the courtyard toward her targets, pretending she was heading for the hedge maze. Soon she was close enough to hear Wong without the aid of a microphone.

"Wait!" the distraught chemist exclaimed, grabbing on to the German's arm. "How do I know you'll destroy the film? Why should I trust you?"

"You have no choice," the blackmailer hissed under his breath. The blonde glared menacingly at Wong, who flinched in response. The man yanked his arm free. "Now control yourself, doctor. And please lower your voice!"

Concerned about being overheard, he looked about—and spotted Sydney approaching them. His brow furrowed and he peered more closely at Sydney's face. *Uh-oh,* she thought, as the German's eerie gold eyes lit up in recognition. *I've been made. But how?*

She had no idea how the German had recognized her, and no time now to figure it out. *"Wir sind nicht allein!"* he barked at his companion. *We are not alone.* He pointed at Sydney. "CIA!"

Letting go of the man's hand, the blonde instantly assumed a defensive posture between Sydney and the German. Heedless of the crowd around her, she dropped to one knee and drew a Glock automatic pistol from her boot. The sight of the weapon provoked shocked gasps and screams from startled civilians. "Go!" the blonde urged the German as she jumped back to her feet. An American accent hinted at Midwestern origins. "I'll take care of this bitch!"

You can try, Sydney thought. She plucked her earring from her right lobe and hurled it like the razor-edged throwing star it actually was. The spinning *shuriken* struck the blonde in the wrist before she could fire her weapon. She yelped in pain as the Glock flew from her fingers and clattered onto the pavement several feet away.

Pandemonium erupted in the plaza as the situation rapidly spiraled out of control. Panicked tourists fled the scene, shouting in alarm. Sydney had to jump backward to avoid being run over by an old man on a scooter, while a running teenager accidentally kicked the fallen pistol under some bushes. Her face pale, Yvonne Wong joined the frantic exodus, hurrying away from the meeting place. The German darted into the entrance of the hedge maze, only to hesitate and look back at his blond accomplice. "Kimber?" he called out, clearly reluctant to leave her behind. *"Eile! Kommen Sie mit mir!"*

"Just keep going!" she insisted. Biting down on her lip, she yanked the silver star from her wrist and hurled it back at Sydney with her other hand. Blood streamed from the gash, but the lack of crimson spray suggested that the throwing star had missed any arteries. The blonde glared murderously at Sydney, who ducked her head to avoid being tagged by the returning *shuriken*. The spinning star whistled past her ear before coming to rest in the trunk of a cherry tree. Sydney was grateful that no innocent bystanders had been in its path.

Clutching her wounded wrist, the blonde turned and followed the German into the maze.

Sydney drew her own gun from her handbag. The loaded Beretta fit her grip perfectly. "You take Wong!" she shouted at Dixon. "I'm going after the other two!"

"Understood!" Dixon replied. Out of the corner of her eye, she saw him turn his hose on the fleeing chemist. A high-pressure stream of water slammed into Wong, knocking her off her feet.

Dixon clutched the grip of the spray nozzle as he rushed toward the downed scientist. Sydney didn't anticipate that her partner would have any trouble subduing Wong.

That's one down, she thought grimly.

She guessed that the other two would not be so easily dealt with. Shedding her handbag, she cautiously entered the maze, only to be confronted with an immediate choice between two hedge-lined passageways. She mentally kicked herself for not familiarizing herself with the layout of the maze while prepping for this operation. Did the German and his Kimber already know the fastest route through the maze?

Probably, she figured. *After all, they chose this site for the meeting.*

She furrowed her brow in frustration. Which way to go? She couldn't afford to waste time exploring the maze, not while the unidentified German was still in possession of that computer disk. It was vital that she recover the formula, whatever that might happen to be. The bad guys had gone to too much trouble to get their hands on it for it to be anything less than a matter of national security.

But how she was supposed to track them through the maze of flora?

She looked quickly for any telltale bloodstains, but the blonde had not left a gory trail behind. *She must have stanched the bleeding somehow,* Sydney guessed. Another thought occurred to her, and she spoke urgently into her communicator. "Phoenix to Merlin, I need a hand here."

"Copy that, Phoenix," Marshall Flinkman replied from APO headquarters, more than three thousand miles away. She visualized the diminutive op-tech specialist seated in front of his computer screens back at the office. "What's the scoop?"

Sydney got right to the point. "I need you to talk me through the hedge maze here at Edgewood Gardens. Can you call up a diagram or aerial photos or something? I need a guide ASAP."

Her foot tapped impatiently against the gravel pathway. Every minute she waited, the greater the odds were that the German and Kimber would escape with the formula.

"No problemo," Marshall assured her. "Just give me a second here." She heard him tapping away at a keyboard in the background. "Okay, got it! I found some old satellite surveillance photos. You're at the start of the maze, right?"

Sydney was impressed—but not too surprised—by how quickly Marshall had located the necessary information. His APO call sign was well chosen; when he had to, Merlin could work magic with computers. "Roger that. Which way?"

"Left," he began. "Then take a sharp right at the next turn."

That was all she needed to hear. Sydney started running down the left-hand corridor before Marshall even finished his sentence. She held her Beretta in front of her as she sprinted through the narrow passageways, rounding the corners as swiftly as safety allowed. Despite the need for haste, she remained on guard, all too aware that Kimber or the German could be waiting to ambush her around every turn. She tried to peer through the verdant greenery, but the dense hedge walls were too thick to see through.

Like an angel on her shoulder, Marshall guided her through the maze, feeding her directions at every intersection. Sydney was grateful for his assistance; she could see how easily one could get lost amid all the bewildering twists and turns. Once, she thought she heard muffled footsteps pounding deeper within the maze, and she longed for a machete so she could hack a straight path through the brush.

Even with Marshall's help, this was taking too long.

Scooting around another corner, she came upon a motionless figure lying prone upon the gravel in front of her. "Hang on, Marshall!" she blurted out as she skidded to a halt in front of the body. Grass-stained yellow coveralls identified the casualty as one of Edgewood's gardeners. She dropped to the man's side and hastily checked his pulse. To her relief, he was only unconscious, not dead. She felt a swollen bump at the back of the gardener's head. The German's handiwork, or Kimber's?

Sydney remembered the blonde's bulging biceps and guessed the latter.

She quickly scoped out the scene. Freshly trimmed branches suggested that the man had been pruning the hedges when attacked by the fugitives. Sydney noted that the gardener's shears were missing.

That's not good, she realized.

"Phoenix?" Anxiety raised Marshall's voice a couple of octaves. "Everything okay over there? You still reading me?"

"I'm fine, Merlin." Satisfied that the waylaid

gardener was not in need of immediate medical attention, she rose to her feet and turned her focus back to the chase. *I'll have to make sure someone calls a doctor after all this is over,* she thought; she hated to leave the poor guy behind, but countless lives could be at stake if the mysterious formula fell into the wrong hands. "Which way now?"

"Er, two rights and a left," Marshall told her. "You're nearing the end of the maze, by the way. There's an enclosed garden with an exit on the other side."

"Glad to hear it," she said, sprinting away from the downed gardener. *Then again,* she realized, *if Kimber wants to ambush me, she's going to have to do it soon.* "Merlin, you mentioned satellite photos before. Any chance you can divert a spy satellite to give you a real-time view from above?"

"Already on it, Phoenix." The sound of rapid-fire tapping came over the comm-link. "Eureka! Big Brother is watching you even as we speak."

Sydney offered a silent prayer of thanks for the clear blue sky above her. Heavy clouds or fog would have interfered with Marshall's ability to scan the maze ahead of her. "Any unpleasant surprises coming up?"

"Let me see," he murmured. Marshall had a tendency to ramble sometimes, but not when her life or a mission was at stake. "Ohmigod, there's someone waiting just around the next corner . . . and, boy, is she hot!"

Bingo, Sydney thought. She slowed to a trot as she neared the next turn. Her finger tensed on the trigger of her gun, but she was reluctant to fire blindly through the hedge wall. What if she missed Kimber and shot an innocent civilian instead? The neatly trimmed yews weren't exactly bulletproof. Besides, she couldn't risk killing the blonde before they had a chance to interrogate her—especially if the German evaded capture. *We'll have to do this the hard way.*

She waited until she was at the very end of the corridor, facing another two-way intersection, then crouched down and somersaulted around the corner. The stolen garden shears jabbed at the air above her, right where her throat should have been, as Kimber lunged forward with an angry grunt. Sydney tumbled past her, than sprang to her feet a few yards beyond the murderous blonde.

"Damn it!" Kimber swore. Momentum carried her forward, almost toppling her onto her face, but she regained her balance and spun around to confront Sydney, shears in hand. A silk handkerchief was wrapped tightly around her injured wrist. Anger flashed in her eyes and rage contorted her exquisite features. "CIA slut! I'll cut you to pieces!"

"Freeze!" Sydney shouted back, drawing a bead on Kimber with her Beretta. Glancing around quickly, she found herself in a topiary garden right outside the maze. High yew walls enclosed the garden, which held a collection of bristling green bushes sculpted into whimsical shapes. Evergreen hippos and lions cavorted in place, along with large geometric cones and pyramids. "Don't move a muscle!"

Her Beretta gave her the upper hand, but what about the German? As far as Sydney knew, he still had the disk with the formula on it, which made him her primary target. The blonde was just a homicidal distraction. *Can I restrain her before her partner gets away for good?*

"Phoenix to Outrigger," she began, hoping Dixon was available to head off the German. Both her gaze and her gunsight remained fixed on Kimber. "Male target remains at large. Immediate interception required. Merlin, can you pinpoint his location?"

Before either of her fellow agents could respond, a harsh voice seized her attention.

"Sydney Bristow!"

Hearing her real name sent a jolt through her system. Looking away from Kimber, she turned to the right and saw the German step out from behind a life-size topiary hippopotamus. A blue-steel revolver glinted in his hand. "Let her go, American whore!"

Despite his warning, he didn't give her a chance to comply with his demand. A shot rang out, and Sydney felt a bullet whiz by her head, missing her by inches. She fired back at the German, who ducked behind the evergreen hippo for cover. He shot at her through the bush, forcing Sydney to seek shelter behind a large green cone the size of a tepee. The German's bullets tore through the dubious protection of the shrub. Shredded branches and pine needles pelted Sydney's face.

Kimber saw her opportunity. Holding the pointed shears above her head, she charged at Sydney from the right. The flaxen-haired Amazon had at least two inches and maybe twenty pounds on her opponent, but Sydney's reflexes were faster. She heard Kimber coming, even over the sharp report of the gunshots, and let her Krav Maga training take over. At the last minute, just as the blonde was bearing down on her, she jumped backward, out of the way of the strike, and thrust her right leg out in front of the other woman's legs.

Kimber went flying. A grunt of pain escaped her lips as she slammed face-first onto the grassy floor of the garden, just beyond the perimeter of the cone-shaped bush. Sydney watched her land and braced herself for the blonde's counterattack. Chances were, Sydney had just made her angrier.

"Phoenix?" Dixon's voice, filled with alarm, came over her comm-link. "I hear gunshots. Please report!"

"I'm still in one piece, Outrigger. So far."

"Understood," he replied tersely. "I'm on my way!"

To Sydney's surprise, Kimber did not spring up again. A gurgling noise issued from the woman's throat as she rolled weakly onto her back. The blades of the shears were lodged deeply between her breasts, and Sydney realized that Kimber must have fallen onto the point of the weapon. Kimber's trembling fingers groped at the shears, but she lacked the strength to extract the blades from her chest. It would have been a wasted effort anyway. Sydney knew a mortal injury when she saw one.

So did the German. "Kimber!" he cried out in anguish, his head briefly visible above the topiary animal. He stared in horror at his dying companion. *"Liebling!"*

"Make them pay!" she called back to her lover. Bright arterial blood trickled from the corner of her mouth. Her tanned face drained of color. "Make them all pay. . . ."

Her body spasmed once, then went limp and still.

Sydney wasted no time mourning the death of the woman who had just tried to kill her. As far as she was concerned, the blonde had brought her gruesome demise upon herself. *Karma's a bitch.*

The German felt otherwise. "You killed her, Sydney!" He glared at her with hate-filled eyes before ducking back behind the cover of the hippo-shaped hedge. "You killed my Kimber!"

Another blast from his pistol tore through Sydney's own topiary, forcing her to crouch down behind the shrub in hopes of presenting a smaller target. *That was a close one,* she thought. She fired back at him, but couldn't tell if she hit him or not. Hidden behind their respective bushes, they were both shooting blindly at each other. The German had the advantage, though, in that he wasn't worried about a stray shot hitting someone outside the garden. If only the hedge walls provided more protection.

At least I've got him pinned down for the moment, Sydney thought. "Merlin, I can't get a visual on the male target. Can you assist?"

"I'm trying, S—Phoenix!" Marshall stammered. His near slip indicated that he knew just how precarious her position was. "But he keeps shifting position behind that big shrub. He won't stay still!"

Sydney exhaled, frustrated. By the time Marshall told her where to aim, the German would have moved again.

A bullet whizzed past her shoulder in a explosion of pine needles. She realized that it was only a matter of time before one of the German's wild shots struck home; the only question was whether Dixon would reach the scene first. "Outrigger, the female target is down, but I am under fire from the male. Please respond!"

"Hang on, Phoenix!" He was breathing hard, as though running at top speed. Sydney heard his shoes pound rapidly against the pavement. She guessed that he was trying to approach the German from the other end of the garden. "I'm coming around the outside of the maze now."

Make it quick, Sydney thought. She fired a warning shot high above the walls of the garden. "Give it up!" she shouted at the German. "My people are closing in. Don't force us to kill you."

"Like you killed Kimber?" A blast of red-hot lead chipped away at the topiary cone, less than six inches away from her face. The German's voice was hoarse with emotion. "I only wish I had time to make you suffer before you die, Sydney!"

How the hell does he know my name? she wondered. That question was almost as scary as his flying bullets. Multiple aliases guarded her true identity, and for good reason. *Have we clashed before?*

Footsteps sounded by the rear entrance to the garden. Sydney peered cautiously around the conical bush, hoping to see her fellow agent arrive to provide some much-needed reinforcement. Between the two of them, they should be able to force the German out from behind the cover of the hippo topiary, and perhaps even induce him to surrender. One way or another, they needed to get that illicit computer disk back.

"Outrigger? Is that you?"

To her horror, a smiling, twentysomething couple entered the topiary garden, seemingly oblivious to the gunshots echoing across the enclosed arboretum. Sydney started to call out a warning, then saw the man signing enthusiastically to the woman. *Oh, God,* Syd realized, aghast. *They're deaf!*

Unaware that they were walking into a gunfight, the pair strolled blithely across the garden. Then the woman spotted Kimber's body lying on the manicured lawn, with a pair of bloody shears jutting from her chest. The female tourist's mouth opened in a silent scream and she pointed frantically at the corpse. Her companion's eyes widened in shock. He stepped between the woman and the body, trying to shield her from the sight. Sydney prayed that they would run like mad from the scene, but instead they seemed frozen in place.

Get out of here! she thought desperately. *It's not safe!*

They never had a chance. The German's gun

blared, and the deaf man stiffened as a bullet slammed into his back. He reached out for the woman, only to topple to the ground. Blood spurted from an exit wound between his ribs. An incoherent moan broke the silence. His horrified companion looked like she couldn't believe what had just taken place before her eyes.

"Paging Nurse Bristow!" the German taunted Sydney. "Your patient requires immediate assistance!"

Bastard! Sydney thought. She realized that the German had shot the innocent man on purpose to keep her occupied while he made a break for it. He had her number, though; there was no way she could let the injured man bleed to death right in front of her. Bolting from behind the conical hedge, she rushed to the victim's side. The deaf woman was already there, sobbing hysterically, as she tried in vain to hold back the blood gushing from his wound. Sydney glimpsed a wedding ring beneath the gore on the woman's hands.

"Merlin, I have a civilian down! Call 911 right away!"

The distraught wife looked up at Sydney. Her tearful eyes implored her, until they spotted the

Beretta in Sydney's grip. Sydney quickly laid the gun aside and shook her head. She signed hastily to the woman, insisting she only wanted to help. "It will be all right," she said aloud, more for her own benefit than the other woman's. Her concerned expression got the message across. "Help is on the way."

Footsteps pounded on the grass. Sydney glanced away from the victim long enough to see the German dash back into the maze. She half-expected him to take one last shot at her with his pistol, but he must have taken her warning about reinforcements seriously. Escape had taken priority over revenge. "Until next time, Agent Bristow!" he hollered back at her as he disappeared into the twisting labyrinth. "Give my regards to Arvin Sloane!"

Sloane? He knows Sloane, too?

Frustration churned within Sydney. However, she had no choice but to let the German get away . . . for now. Giving the bleeding tourist her full attention, she tore open the man's shirt to get a better look at his injuries. A pink froth bubbled up from the wound, indicating that the bullet had nicked one of the man's lungs. She had to admire the German's precision. The wound was life-threatening, but not instantly fatal: just the thing to keep her by the man's side while the nameless blackmailer escaped. A puddle of blood spread out beneath the victim's body. His face took on a grayish tint as he gasped for breath.

"Phoenix?" Dixon came charging into the garden from the opposite direction. He was too well trained to use her real name in public, even under such dire circumstances. His dark eyes scanned the site as he held up his gun with both hands. The topiary displays blocked his view. "What is your position?"

"Over here!" Sydney called out.

Dixon rushed to where she was kneeling. He dropped beside the victim, next to the man's wife. "Good Lord," he said softly at the sight of so much innocent blood. He glanced around warily for any potential threats. "The shooter?"

"Gone," Sydney said grimly.

Dixon nodded. He didn't question Sydney's decision to see to the injured civilian instead of pursuing the German. She knew he would have done the same in her situation. The bleeding man looked like he was on the brink of death. "What do we have here?"

"A sucking chest wound, plus an entry wound in the back. I could use some help." Sydney reached beneath the man, cautiously checking to make sure his spine was intact. Thankfully, the bullet seemed to have missed his vertebrae. "We need to turn him onto his side."

"Let's do it." He gently eased the man's wife aside, while Sydney applied pressure to the exit wound. Air whistled through her clasped fingers. Dixon placed his hands underneath the man. "On my count. One, two . . . three!"

In a smooth motion Dixon lifted the wounded man onto his side. To Sydney's relief, the victim's ragged breathing grew steadier now that his good lung had been elevated. Blood soaked through the knees of Dixon's yellow overalls as he applied pressure to the entry wound in the man's back.

That's better, Sydney thought. The poor guy was still in bad shape, but at least they had halted the massive hemorrhaging for the time being. Now all they had to do was keep him alive until the EMTs showed up—which ought to be any minute. Sydney thought she heard a helicopter flying toward them.

The victim's wife looked on anxiously. Her

hands and clothes were stained with her husband's blood. Sydney remembered finding the lifeless body of her fiancé, so many years ago, and felt a stab of intense sympathy for the woman. She wished she could promise that her husband was going to be okay, but there were no guarantees. At least he had a chance. No thanks to that German son of a bitch.

She tried not to think about the missing disk.

FORTY-EIGHT HOURS LATER

Sydney and her fellow agents sat around the pristine white table in the APO briefing room, waiting for an update on the Yvonne Wong affair. Frosted glass walls, with sleek white trim, gave the room a cool, antiseptic feel. You'd never guess that the modern-looking chamber, along with the adjoining hallways and cubicles, was hidden deep beneath the L.A. subway system. Authorized Personnel Only was the code name for the black-ops unit also known as APO, and that term accurately described the men and women currently assembled.

"The deceased female operative has been identified as Kimber Gill," Arvin Sloane announced from the head of the table. Clad in a dapper gray suit, he presided over the briefing as head of APO. He clicked a remote and photos of the deadly blonde, both pre- and post-mortem, appeared on video screens built into the wall. Sydney recalled the woman's grisly demise and shuddered. "She was an American-born anarchist, believed to be the chief bodyguard—and mistress—of this man."

He clicked the remote again. Sydney's photos of the male blackmailer took over the screens, alongside other surveillance photos taken on previous occasions. Sydney recognized the man's shaggy features and creepy yellow eyes. Her jaw tightened as she recalled the callous way the German had gunned down an innocent civilian. That his victim was now resting in a hospital, not in a grave, did little to cool the anger simmering inside her. *Next time, you're not getting away from me,* she vowed. *No matter what.*

"Oskar Murnau," Sloane continued, attaching a name to the object of Syd's animosity. "Formerly of the East German secret police. After the fall of the Berlin Wall, he entered the private sector as a high-ranking member of the Alliance." Sloane did not have to remind anyone at the table that he had also been part of the Alliance, a now-defunct criminal organization that had once profited from international arms and intelligence trading. Every agent at APO was all too aware of their leader's sinister past—and few of them believed that he had truly reformed. "As a member of the Board of Twelve, he had full access to the files of all SD cells . . . at least, until he was drummed out of the Alliance some time later."

So that's how he knew me, Sydney realized. She had spent several years working for Arvin Sloane at SD-6, falsely believing it to be a legitimate arm of the CIA. That she now found herself working for Arvin Sloane once more, this time on the right side of the law, was an irony she lived with every day. *Murnau must have seen photos of me in the Alliance's files. He also must have found out about my role in bringing them down.*

"Why was he expelled from the Alliance?" Jack Bristow asked. Sydney's father sat across the table from her, wearing a conservative black suit. His lean, clean-shaven face maintained a characteristically aloof expression.

"Differing philosophies," Sloane replied. "Murnau is rabidly anti-American, blaming the U.S. for the collapse of his old regime in East Germany. Ultimately, he proved more interested in outright terrorism than the steady acquisition of wealth and power. Put bluntly, he was a loose cannon—with an insatiable appetite for acts of wanton destruction. In some circles he is known as Der Werwolf, due to his penchant for staging his terrorist attacks only during full moons."

"Wow. How creepy is that?" Marshall asked rhetorically. The brainy little tech guy peered at the photos of Murnau on display. He fidgeted in his seat, full of nervous energy. "Although, there have been some intriguing studies linking antisocial behavior to the lunar cycle. Who knows? Maybe the full moon exerts some kind of a tidal effect on the human endocrine system. . . ."

"More likely, the moon possesses some deep personal symbolism to Murnau," Jack stated, cutting off Marshall's rambling. "It's possible that we may be able to use this psychological quirk to our advantage."

Sydney recalled Der Werwolf's vengeful reaction to his mistress's death. *Just what I need,* she thought, *another lunatic out for my blood.*

"Do we know yet what was on that computer disk Murnau escaped with?" Michael Vaughn asked. Beneath the table her boyfriend gave Sydney's hand a reassuring squeeze, just to let her know that he wasn't blaming her for Murnau's escape.

She glanced at his lean, Gallic face, seeing only professionalism in his cool demeanor. She didn't mind his bringing up the subject of the disk. It was vital that they find out what sort of data Murnau had extracted from Yvonne Wong.

Sloane's own expression darkened. "Under interrogation, Dr. Wong has confessed to providing Murnau with the top-secret formula to Black Thorine."

"You're kidding!" Eric Weiss blurted out. The portly agent sat on the opposite side of the table, next to Sydney's half sister, Nadia. "That is serious bad news."

Tell me about it, Sydney thought. Black Thorine was a chemical explosive of unparalleled power. She and Nadia had recovered a stolen quantity of the substance from a Russian arms dealer only a few months before. A CIA strike team had later destroyed the secret Ukrainian laboratory where the illegal (and undetectable) explosive had been manufactured. *I thought we were done with that stuff.*

She and Nadia exchanged a worried look. Neither of them had forgotten just how dangerous Black Thorine was. One drop was enough to level an entire city block.

And now Murnau had the formula.

"Does Wong have any idea what Murnau wanted the formula for?" Dixon asked. Sydney could tell that he was also troubled by the prospect of a man like Murnau gaining the ability to manufacture Black Thorine. With two young children to worry about, he had a very personal stake in the war against terror.

Sloane shook his head. "Wong was not privy to Murnau's ultimate agenda. All she cared about was hiding her own dirty little secret." Contempt dripped from his voice. "Given Murnau's anti-American proclivities, we have to assume that he is planning a major terrorist strike against this country, employing Black Thorine as a weapon." He walked around the table, handing out dossiers to the seated agents. "Finding Murnau has just become our top priority. Trust me, I know this man—he's a true fanatic."

Sydney shuddered at the thought of a terrorist mastermind whom Arvin Sloane, of all people, considered a dangerous fanatic. . . .

CHAPTER 2

APO BUNKER
LOS ANGELES
ONE MONTH LATER

Weeks after the incident at the gardens, Sydney found herself no closer to tracking Murnau down. She glanced at her desk calendar. The next full moon was only six days away. Would Murnau have succeeded in manufacturing Black Thorine by then?

Maybe not, she thought, *but we can't take that chance.*

Sydney's workstation was located in a cubicle outside Sloane's office. She sat in front of her computer screen, tuning out the buzz of activity coming from the rest of the underground facility. A family portrait, taken before her mother's supposed death, occupied a place of honor on her desktop, next to framed photos of Vaughn and Nadia. A menu for her favorite take-out sushi place was tacked to the bulletin board. Air-conditioning kept the hidden bunker comfortably cool.

Murnau's file occupied her monitor. Sydney sipped from a cup of hot tea as she reviewed the German terrorist's dossier for perhaps the hundredth time. According to reliable sources, Murnau had been linked to the bombing of a U.S. embassy in New Zealand, the crash of an American passenger jet, the mass slaughter of a Congressional fact-finding junket in the former Yugoslavia, and numerous other atrocities. And that wasn't even counting his prior career as an officer in the Stasi, the dreaded East German secret police. Even then, Der Werwolf had enjoyed a reputation for heart-lessness and brutality.

Unfortunately, nothing in his bio offered any hint as to his present whereabouts and/or future objectives. To her frustration, Sydney saw that nearly all of Murnau's known associates were dead or missing.

Including Kimber Gill.

Murnau's file confirmed the intimate relationship between the terrorist and his Amazonian bodyguard. Sydney wished that she could have taken Kimber alive; no doubt she would have been a font of information on her lover's activities, once she had been made to talk. *Instead, all I did was make a personal enemy out of Murnau himself.*

Discouraged, and needing a break, she closed Murnau's file and called up the morning news instead. Her job required that she keep abreast of current events, both locally and abroad, so she rationalized that she wasn't really shirking her duty.

A headline on the *Los Angeles Times* Web site caught her eye, and she clicked on the link:

DEATH AT LA BREA

Murdered Woman Dumped at Tar Pits

WILSHIRE BOULEVARD—Students on a fourth-grade field trip to the La Brea Tar Pits were shocked to discover the body of a recently murdered woman mired in the mucky pool at the corner of Wilshire and Curson. A volunteer guide immediately summoned the police to the site, which is better known as a repository of prehistoric fossils.

The victim has been identified as Christiana Stephens, 31. The freelance graphic designer had not been reported missing before the discovery of the body. No cause of death has been released, but a police spokesman confirms that the death is being investigated as a homicide.

Bizarre, Sydney thought. She had seen plenty of weird stuff in her career, but the story still struck her as unusually grotesque. It had been years since she'd visited the tar pits, yet she retained fond memories of childhood excursions to the celebrated tourist attraction. She felt sorry for the poor kids who had stumbled onto the body, and hoped that emotional counseling was being provided for the children.

Her gaze remained glued to the screen. Something about the story sent a peculiar chill down her spine. Was it just that the murdered woman was nearly the same age as her, or something more? She read over the article one more time. The victim's name, Christiana Stephens, tugged on her memory.

Where have I heard that name?

Marshall strolled by her cubicle, humming the theme from *Star Wars*.

"Hey, Marshall," she called out to him. "Do you have a second?"

He came to a stop and backed up into her workspace. "Sure. What's up?"

"Does the name Christiana Stephens mean anything to you?"

"Hmm. That does sound familiar." His sizable brow furrowed as he searched his photographic memory. His eyes lit up and he snapped his fingers. "Got it! That's one of your old aliases, remember? From that mission in Geneva, when you broke into that safety-deposit box to get Ineni Hassan's account number."

Of course! Sydney thought. She had posed as Christiana Stephens, a fictional diamond dealer, in order to gain access to the Swiss bank account of a suspected arms dealer. That was way back in her SD-6 days, nearly six years ago.

She was vaguely embarrassed not to have placed the name on her own. *Then again,* she reminded herself, *I've used dozens of different aliases over the years. I can't be expected to remember them all.*

Can I?

"Why do you ask?" Marshall inquired. She gestured at the computer monitor and he read the unsettling news item over her shoulder. "Oh, geez, that's no good. I've been meaning to take little Mitchell to the tar pits." Looking away from the screen, he gazed anxiously at Sydney. "This is probably just a coincidence, right?"

"Maybe," she said dubiously. An awful suspicion crept up on her. "How hard would it be to check out some of my other old aliases?"

An apprehensive look came over Marshall's face. "Step aside," he sighed, and Sydney willingly surrendered her seat in front of the computer. She suspected she could conduct the same Web searches herself, but Marshall would surely locate any relevant data faster. For her own peace of mind, she needed to know the truth as quickly as possible. One way or another.

Please let me be wrong about this, she prayed silently. Maybe Marshall was right and this really was just a coincidence. Christiana Stephens wasn't such an uncommon name; it wasn't surprising that it belonged to a real person. There were probably plenty of women by that name. *But how many of them have ended up dead in a tar pit?*

Marshall cracked his knuckles before resting his fingers upon the keyboard. "Do you have any particular alias in mind?"

"Start with the old SD-6 missions, around the same time as the Hassan assignment." *That was not long after I discovered the truth about SD-6,* she recalled, *and started working as a double agent for the CIA.*

Could there be a connection?

"Okay," he replied. Marshall had been around during those days as well. Sloane had pretty much re-created the core of the old SD-6 here at APO.

The more things change . . .

She held her breath as Marshall swiftly compiled a list of her aliases from that era. The false identities triggered a flood of memories in Sydney: she recalled perilous exploits all around the globe. Conspicuously missing were the aliases she had employed while moonlighting for the CIA. That was a different set of files.

"How about we start with Kate Jones?" he suggested.

Now that she knew what the context was, she

instantly placed the name. Kate Jones was the alias she had adopted while posing as an American tourist in Morocco, in order to spy on a meeting taking place between a notorious terrorist leader and an industrial demolitions specialist. Information obtained from that assignment had allowed her to avert an attack on an international trade conference, but she hadn't used the alias since.

"You know, that's a pretty generic name," Marshall stalled. He seemed hesitant to begin, as if fearful of what they might find. His fingers hovered above the keyboard.

"Do it," she told him.

Reluctantly, he went to work. Sydney watched intently as he surfed the Web like the pro that he was. Text and images flashed across the screen faster than she could keep up with them. She crossed her fingers, hoping against hope that this was all a wild goose chase.

Maybe I'm just being paranoid.

No such luck. Marshall's dancing fingers slowed to a crawl and he clicked on one last link. He winced at the news item his search had turned up. "Oh, hell," he said in a hushed tone.

Sydney read the story over his shoulder.

MURDERED WOMAN LEFT AT BUS STOP

LOS ANGELES—The body of Katherine Jones, 30, was found early yesterday morning at a bus stop near the intersection of West Sixth Street and Whittier Boulevard. The victim of an apparent homicide, Jones was seated on a public bench, as though waiting for the #18 bus line. Police discovered exact change for a bus fare tucked into the body's right hand. Early-morning commuters were startled to find Jones's remains when they arrived at the bus stop around 6 A.M.

"Someone has a sick sense of humor," stated one of the investigating officers, who asked to remain anonymous. "He propped her up like a goddamn mannequin."

A local resident, Jones was employed as a high school English teacher. She is survived by a husband and a six-year-old daughter.

No suspects have been arrested in connection with the crime.

A photo of Kate Jones, perhaps obtained from a relative, accompanied the article. The black-and-white portrait showed a smiling young woman, not unlike Sydney in age and appearance, who had no idea her life would soon be tragically cut short. Sydney's heart sank as she contemplated the news item, which seemed to confirm her worst suspicions. Checking the date, she saw that Jones had been killed nearly a month ago, less than a week after Murnau had escaped from Sydney at Edgewood Gardens.

Could Der Werwolf be responsible?

"Statistically speaking, this is kind of alarming," Marshall said. "Two dead women, each of whom happens to share a name with one of your past aliases, both turning up dead in the past few weeks? I don't like the sound of this."

Tell me about it, Sydney thought. A disturbing picture was definitely forming. "What's the next name on the list?"

Marshall worked through the list with dismaying ease. Less than an hour later, an unmistakable pattern had emerged:

Molly Zerdin, thirty-one. Found hanging from a lamppost on the Venice boardwalk. Sydney had posed as a Molly Zerdin six years before, on assignment in Oxford, England.

Christina Auriti, thirty. Found stuffed into a

trash bin on Rodeo Drive. Not to be confused with Christina Auriti of Auriti Antiquities, Sydney's cover in Mexico City during the Rambaldi clock affair.

Four women dead, Sydney counted. *In less than a month.* She felt sick to her stomach. There was no way to deny the awful truth.

Someone is killing my namesakes.

CHAPTER 3

"Are you certain about this?" Sloane asked.

Red leather upholstery provided the only spots of color in his office, which was dominated by glass panels with white trim. Electronic monitors were installed in the walls, within easy view of his clear glass desk. An illuminated world map monitored hot spots throughout the globe. Printouts of the relevant news articles were spread out on the desktop. Sydney and Marshall stood in front of the desk, having come straight from her cubicle, while her father stood stiffly beside Sloane, looking over the documents as well. A scowl betrayed Jack's concern over all that the printouts implied.

"It's right there in black and white," Sydney insisted. "Four incidents in four weeks."

"Plus, it's not just the names," Marshall added. "I checked, and all four victims match Sydney's approximate age and appearance. We're talking young Caucasian women, roughly thirty years old. Of course, none of them are quite as attractive as the real thing"—he glanced sheepishly at Sydney. "If you wanted to put together a lineup of Sydney impersonators, you could do worse than pick these four women."

"The evidence *is* provocative," Jack conceded. "What about the rest of SD-6? Have you checked Dixon's former aliases? Or my own?"

"I'm way ahead of you, Mr. Bristow," Marshall said. "I ran a search of some other phony names from the good old bad-pretending-to-be-good days, but no one else's aliases were associated with murder and mayhem . . . except, that is, for the stuff we did ourselves." Sloane cleared his throat ominously, and Marshall got to the point. "The killer seems to be targeting just Sydney's past aliases."

"Isn't that enough?" she exclaimed. "This is a

nightmare. These woman are being killed because of me!"

"You can't blame yourself," her father assured her. "Those aliases were not deliberately based on real people. The idea was simply to choose commonplace names that would not call attention to themselves. There were bound to be civilians with the same names." His voice was uncharacteristically gentle. "There are millions of people in the greater Los Angeles area alone. We could hardly eliminate all those names as potential aliases."

I know that, Sydney thought. But she couldn't stand the idea that innocent women were being killed just because she had inadvertently borrowed their names in the past. "We have to do something about this!"

"Such as?" Sloane asked. He leaned back against the deep red cushions of his chair. "These murders are certainly troubling, but this strikes me as a matter for the police. Given the age and obsolete nature of the aliases involved, there's no evidence that our current operations are compromised. More important, I'm reluctant to commit vital resources to investigating these incidents, especially while Oskar Murnau remains at large."

Sydney couldn't believe her ears. "You can't be serious. Don't you realize what this means?" She gestured violently at the news clippings. "This could be just the beginning. Think of all the aliases I employed in my SD-6 days alone. Dozens of other women could be in danger!"

"And thousands of lives could be lost if Murnau synthesizes enough Black Thorine to stage a major attack on the United States." Sloane appeared unmoved by Sydney's emotional outburst. He neatly gathered the papers on his desk and handed them back to her. "APO was formed to deal with matters of national security. I appreciate that these tragic events have affected you on a personal level, but finding Murnau has to remain our top priority. We can't afford to be distracted by a time-consuming manhunt for a mere serial killer. That's what the police and FBI are for."

Sydney refused to take the documents back from Sloane. "But what if Murnau is behind these murders as well? As revenge for the death of Kimber Gill?" She was grasping at straws, desperate to convince Sloane to take the killings seriously. "The first murder took place less than a week after the incident at Edgewood."

Her eyes turned toward her father, begging him for assistance. Jack had known Sloane for more than thirty years, ever since the two men had served in the CIA together back in the 1970s. If anybody could get through to Sloane, it was her father.

"Sydney may have a point," Jack observed. "We can't know for certain that Murnau played a part in these killings, but it would be unwise to dismiss that possibility entirely." His voice took on a graver tone. "In any event, I'm uncomfortable knowing that an unknown party is this familiar with one of our agent's former aliases. These murders could be seen as an implied threat against Sydney's life."

Sloane frowned, but he appeared to take Jack's words under consideration. He leafed through the documents one more time.

"Very well," he said finally. "I'll assign Nadia and Weiss to look into this matter. Nevertheless, I expect the rest of this organization to remain focused on the task of locating Oskar Murnau and recovering the formula for Black Thorine—before he has the opportunity to wreak havoc on this country." Sloane stared pointedly at Sydney. As usual, his cold, shrewd eyes made her skin crawl. "Am I making myself understood?"

"Of course," Sydney said. She shot her father a grateful look, then decided to press her luck a bit further. "All things considered, though, I would like to pursue this investigation myself. Perhaps Nadia can be kept on the Murnau case instead?"

Sydney had plenty of faith in her sister's abilities, but she wasn't sure she could live with herself if she didn't personally do everything she could to halt the killings. *It's the least I can do for those women who are dead because of me.*

"Absolutely not." Sloane shook his head. "With all due respect to my daughter and Agent Weiss, you have more field experience than either of them. I need my top agents concentrating on the search for Murnau, not diverted by what is most likely a sideshow." Sydney opened her mouth to protest, but Sloane held up his hand to cut her off. "In addition, you have also had firsthand dealings with Murnau."

Sydney was not about to give up so easily. "But Murnau already knows what I look like. Wouldn't it be better to assign an agent he will be less likely to recognize? Someone like Nadia? She never worked for SD-6."

"I have made my decision, Agent Bristow." A frosty tone entered Sloane's voice. He took the folder on the killings and decisively dropped it into a file drawer. "The more you argue with me, the more you convince me that you are too emotionally involved to investigate these murders objectively." He brusquely turned his attention to the other papers waiting on his desk. Declining to make eye contact, he gestured toward the exit. "Thank you for calling this matter to my attention. Please ask Agents Weiss and Santos to step into my office."

"Yes, sir!" Marshall chirped. He looked anxious to get back to his lab and away from the tension in the room.

Sydney hesitated, reluctant to abandon the fight, but her father signaled her to back off. Trusting his judgment, especially where Sloane was concerned, she turned around and followed Marshall out the door. She hoped she was making the right move.

Instinctively, she looked for Vaughn, then remembered that he was pursuing leads in Berlin. So far his personal connections in the German intelligence community had failed to turn up any clues to Murnau's current whereabouts, and

Sydney missed his comforting presence.

I could really use someone to talk to right now.

Her father joined her in the corridor outside Sloane's office. "Thanks for backing me up before," she said sincerely. She wasn't entirely happy with the compromise that had been reached, but at least her dad had managed to persuade Sloane to look into the murders. "I appreciate it."

"You're welcome," Jack said stiffly. Expressions of emotion tended to make him uncomfortable. He made sure the door to Sloane's office was shut. "I was being honest when I said that these murders worry me." He glanced around to make sure that they were not being overheard, then lowered his voice. "I want you to know that I intend to track down this killer quietly, using my own resources."

Sydney was not surprised by his statement. She knew how far he was willing to go to protect her. "Let me know if there's anything I can do to help," she said. Sloane notwithstanding, she didn't intend to stand around waiting for the alias killer to strike again. *I'm going to stop this, no matter what it takes.*

"I want you to move out of your house for the time being." He scribbled an address onto the back of a business card. "There's an apartment in Santa Monica that I set up as an emergency safe house years ago. It's not listed in any government file. Not even Sloane or the CIA know about it. I want you to live there, under an assumed name, until this assassin is neutralized one way or another."

Sydney winced at the thought of taking on another alias. *One thing's for sure,* she resolved. *I'm going to choose a name that's not listed in a single California phone book.*

"Do you think that's necessary?" she asked him.

"Better safe than sorry," he stated bluntly. "At present we have no clear idea as to the full extent of the killer's knowledge. Did you and Marshall check any of your more recent aliases?"

Sydney nodded. "Not all of them, of course. That would take days. But we did some spot checks of aliases both from my stint at the CIA and from my time here at APO. As far as we can tell, none of the later aliases have been targeted." She frowned. "At least, not yet."

"That's encouraging," Jack said. "We should do a more comprehensive search on those aliases later, but it's highly possible that the killer does not know about your current status with APO. Perhaps his intel only covers your activities at SD-6."

Let's hope so, Sydney thought. She had experienced a moment of panic earlier when she'd recalled that she had once used the name of Will Tippin's sister as an alias. Granted, that had been a freelance excursion, unsanctioned by either SD-6 or the CIA, but she had still breathed a sigh of relief to discover that, according to the Internet, Amy Tippin was alive and well. *Still, my list of official SD-6 aliases is long enough to give the killer more than enough targets to keep busy.*

"Why would someone do this?" she asked in frustration. Her fists were clenched at her sides as she and her dad walked back to her cubicle. "Is he murdering these women in hopes of eventually getting to the real me?"

"It's possible, but unlikely," Jack stated. An expert on game theory, he had a singular talent for seeing through the stratagems of others. "The killer obviously has access to an old file on you. It strikes me as improbable that anyone could know so much about your past assignments without also learning your real name and address. More likely, the murders are a form of psychological warfare. Whoever the killer is, he wants to torture you mentally—perhaps for revenge, or perhaps just to put you off your game."

Either way, Sydney thought, *it's working.*

She was appalled by the idea that innocent women were being killed just to mess with her head. "By why the tar pits, or that stunt at the bus stop? Is there some sort of message there that I'm missing?"

"I suspect the idea was simply to guarantee sufficient news coverage." Jack's voice held a note of grudging respect for the murderer's planning. "The killer *wants* you to hear about the killings, and to make the connection between the murders. The whole idea is for you to understand what's happening."

That makes sense, she thought, *in a sick sort of way.* Why else would the killer leave Christiana Stephens's body in the shallow part of the tar pit, where it was sure to be found? "What kind of person would do something like this? Murnau?" She had thrown the terrorist's name at Sloane mostly as a ploy to secure his cooperation, but now she gave the theory more serious consideration. "Do you really think it could be him?"

"Possibly," her father said. "He knows you're

on his trail, and he may want revenge for the death of his mistress. Furthermore, as a former member of the Alliance, he could know enough about your career at SD-6 to compile a list of your aliases from those days."

Sydney felt as though her past had come back to haunt her. "But I don't understand. If he wants revenge, why doesn't he just kill me? He knows my real name. It can't be too hard to find out where I live."

"Killing you would be counterproductive," Jack stated. "Murnau, if he is behind this, must know that your murder would simply focus all of your organization's energies on him. The CIA, or whomever he suspects you may be working for these days, would not rest until they found the killer of one of their top agents. Murnau doesn't want that kind of heat, not when he's planning something big with the Black Thorine. Instead, he may be using these killings to keep you distracted and off balance while he pursues his primary objective. The fact that the murders are certain to upset you may well be a welcome bonus."

Sydney nodded, understanding. *Psychological warfare.* The German's harsh accent echoed in her memory: *"I only wish I had time to make you suffer before you die, Sydney!"*

Was this what he had in mind?

If Murnau *was* playing head games with her, Sydney was determined not to let him get to her. She let her father return to his office, then sat down at her computer. Although the murders preyed on her mind, she forced herself to concentrate on her continuing search for the elusive German terrorist.

Working on the assumption that Murnau was intent on manufacturing Black Thorine now that he had the formula, Sydney had become quite conversant with the chemistry involved. Thankfully, Marshall had thoroughly analyzed the samples of the superexplosive that she and Nadia had obtained earlier in the year, so he had been able to explain the basics to her and suggest a couple of promising avenues of inquiry.

Thorium nitrate, the primary component of Black Thorine, was relatively easy to obtain, being about as common as lead. However, the formula also required several more exotic ingredients, most notably neptunium-237, a rare transuranic element produced as a by-product of commercial nuclear power generation. Because neptunium can be used in nuclear weapons, shipments of the radioactive substance are closely monitored by the Nuclear Regulatory Agency, in compliance with strict export controls mandated by the International Atomic Energy Agency in Vienna. Murnau was going to need large quantities of neptunium to manufacture Black Thorine in bulk. And thanks to the tracking regulations involved, there was little chance that he could obtain the isotope legally. That meant he had to turn to the black market, where Sydney had already set out snares to catch him.

Under the username *tania3000*, Sydney had been prowling online chat rooms and bulletin boards known to be frequented by brokers in restricted materials and equipment. Her persona was that of a black-market dealer with illegal quantities of neptunium to sell. With luck, someone representing Murnau would soon be in touch with her—assuming that the crazed German had not already obtained all the Np-237 he required.

If that's the case, the clock is definitely ticking.

At the same time, under the name *failsafe*, she had also put herself forward as a potential customer looking to score some neptunium under the table, no questions asked. Hopefully, this approach would lead her to the same broker Murnau was dealing with—in time to trace any illicit neptunium shipments to the terrorist's current base of operations.

I have supply and demand covered, she thought optimistically. Under the circumstances, she was grateful that neither of her two new identities had required her to generate an alias of the sort that had doomed her previous namesakes. Forcibly expelling such concerns from her mind, if only for the moment, she went online and logged in as *tania3000. Time to see if anyone has taken the bait.*

The transmission was rerouted via multiple satellites and piggybacked signals, making her actual physical location all but impossible to trace. *Tania3000*'s private in-box held a few inquiries about her alleged neptunium, but none that could have conceivably come from Murnau or his representatives. Instead, she recognized the now familiar handles of a white-supremacist sect in Idaho, a Sri Lankan "charity" with connections to the Tamil Tigers, a Peruvian revolutionary splinter group, and, ironically, an ongoing FBI sting operation. Disappointed, she filed away the incriminating queries for future reference, then logged in as *failsafe*.

At least this sort of electronic espionage doesn't require a change of wigs, she reflected as she struck out once more. No one was interested in hawking any unlicensed Np-237, although she had received numerous offers of Zippe-type nuclear centrifuges, South African vortex tubes, high-density shielding, Nigerian yellowcake, Cray supercomputers, "unbreakable" encryption programs, bubonic plague, sarin gas components, and other assorted varieties of illegal contraband. *Your basic terrorist spam,* she thought in disgust as she reviewed the latest messages. *Nothing that points me toward Murnau.*

Scowling, she reposted her original queries and logged off again. Perhaps her snares would pay off eventually, but for now she felt as though she had hit a dead end. Her father and the rest of APO were pursuing other leads, she knew, but with no greater success. Der Werwolf was keeping a maddeningly low profile.

Unable to sit around doing nothing, she decided

to check with Marshall on a related matter. She lunged from her chair and strode restlessly out into the hall, emerging from her cubicle just in time to see Nadia and Weiss exit Sloane's office. A familiar-looking folder was tucked under Weiss's arm.

"Sydney!" Nadia rushed over to console her. With her dark eyes and hair and her bronzed complexion, Sydney's half sister could often pass as Hispanic, even though she was actually the illegitimate daughter of Arvin Sloane and Irina Derevko, Sydney's Russian mother. Nadia's face radiated concern. "My father was just telling me about these awful murders. You must be devastated!"

"Yeah," Weiss added. A rare frown marred his jovial features. "This whole thing is just twisted, and not in a good way."

Sydney appreciated their sympathy. "I've had better days," she admitted.

"Well, we're on the case," Weiss assured her. "Trust me, we'll get this freak. You can count on us."

But will you get the killer before another poor woman is murdered? Sydney wondered. She considered offering her unsanctioned assistance, as she had with her father, then hesitated. She didn't want to put Nadia in the position of having to circumvent her own father. Despite Sydney's own bitter history with Sloane, she tried not to come between Nadia and her dad, even though this was often easier said than done. *Nadia deserves to know her father, even if he hardly deserves a daughter like her.*

"I know," she said simply. "Thanks."

Nadia gave her an encouraging hug. "If there's anything I can do to help you get through this, just let me know."

A thought occurred to her. "My dad thinks I should relocate to a safe house until we've found the killer. Maybe you should too?"

She and Nadia shared a house a short drive from APO headquarters. Sydney worried that the unknown killer might try to get to her through her sister. *What if he's just warming up with my name-sakes?*

"I'll think about it," Nadia said, letting go of her sister. "Don't worry, though. I can take care of myself."

That's true, Sydney admitted. Nadia had grown up on the streets of Buenos Aires before being recruited by an Argentinean intelligence outfit. She was tougher than she looked. "I know. Anyway, we can talk about this more tonight, while I'm pack-ing," Sydney said. She glanced down the hall at her destination. "Right now I need to talk to Marshall about something."

"We won't keep you, then," Nadia said. She and Weiss headed back toward their respective cubicles. "Just remember, Sydney. This isn't your fault."

Everyone keeps saying that, she thought, *so why don't I believe it?*

She watched her fellow agents depart, then continued on her way. Talking to her sister had lightened her mood, but only for a moment. She hoped Marshall had something that would take her mind off the murders—and help her track down Murnau.

Marshall's lab was tucked away in a corner. Shelves reached to the ceiling, packed with exotic hardware in various states of construction. Wire bins were stacked with spare electrical compo-nents and gizmos. High-powered servers hummed in the background. Photos of his wife and baby son were taped to the corners of a large flat-screen monitor. Blueprints for concealed weapons and miniature X-ray cameras were scribbled on the backs of envelopes and napkins. An Elektra action figure was perched on top of a backup computer monitor. Fast-food wrappers littered the floor. Smoke rose from a heated soldering iron. The air smelled like melted plastic.

The op-tech expert was seated at his cluttered workbench, installing a Taser into a toothbrush, when Sydney appeared in the doorway. "Am I interrupting?" she asked.

"What? No, no . . . of course not." He laid down the red-hot iron and hopped off his stool to greet her. "Come on in. You know you're always welcome here. *Mi casa es su casa.* That's Spanish for 'My house is your house,' although, of course, you already know that. I didn't mean to imply otherwise. I mean, your Spanish is probably *mucho* better than mine. . . ." To her surprise, he seemed to be uncomfortable, staring down at the floor as if reluctant to meet her eyes. "Look, I want to apologize to you . . . for not standing up to Sloane back there in his office. I wanted to take your side—really—but, to tell you the truth, that guy still scares the crap out of me."

As well he should, Sydney thought; she knew better than most people just what Arvin Sloane was capable of. "You don't need to apologize," she insisted. "That was my fight, not yours. Besides, Sloane wasn't entirely wrong. We can't let these murders make us forget about finding Murnau." *Especially if he's the one behind them,* she added silently. "Speaking of whom," she continued, "how are you doing on that Black Thorine detector?"

Besides being amazingly destructive, the top-secret explosive was also supposedly undetectable; this was just one of the reasons why the substance violated at least a dozen international treaties. Yet Sloane had tasked Marshall to come up with some sort of portable device they could use to locate Black Thorine in the field. If and when they ever got a line on Murnau's location, such a device might make the difference between success and a catastrophe of unthinkable proportions.

"I'm glad you asked!" he said, lifting his gaze from the floor. He was visibly relieved to discover that Sydney was not disappointed in him. "That's been an interesting challenge, but I think I'm closing in on a solution." He hopped back onto his stool as he went into his spiel. "As you know, Black Thorine can't be detected by any of the usual means. Sniffers, X-rays, dogs . . . that sort of thing. But researchers at Kansas State University have gotten some encouraging results using gamma rays and neutrons. They beam neutrons into a target area, then detectors monitor the return signals, sort of like a radar gun. But these sensors are linked to computers that can recognize the unique atomic signatures of specific elements."

"Like neptunium-237," Sydney suggested.

"Right!" he confirmed, delighted that she saw where he was going with this. "So far the prototypes in Kansas only have a range of a couple yards, but I think I've figured out some tricks to extend that to a significant degree." He gestured toward a stack of notes being held down by an open can of Jolt cola. The charts and equations were way over Sydney's head. "They're fairly ingenious, if I do say so myself."

"I'm sure," she said. "Do we have an ETA for this gadget?"

Marshall scratched his chin. "Well, the biggest problem is coming up with a portable version. It's not going to be easy shrinking the whole setup down to a handheld unit." He took a sip of his soda. "Just give me a couple more days, and a few massive doses of caffeine, and I should have something for you."

"Thanks, Marshall," Sydney said. "Anything you can do to speed things up will be greatly appreciated." She hated to put any extra pressure on him, but time was of the essence. Besides the urgency of the threat posed by Murnau, Sydney had another factor weighing on her mind. The sooner she could bring in the German, the sooner she could give her full attention to the alias killings.

But how many women would die in the meantime?

CHAPTER 4

LOS ANGELES

A knock on the door caught Jack Bristow by surprise.

The veteran agent seldom entertained visitors at his home. Jack valued his privacy, all the more so because his personal security was so often a matter of life and death. Over three decades in the spy trade he had made a lot of enemies.

He instantly went on alert, drawing a Glock 17 automatic from his shoulder holster. He rose from the black leather couch where he had been researching the alias killings. Classified files, several of which he was not technically entitled to have in his possession, were organized neatly on a glass-topped coffee table in front of the couch.

With his gun at the ready, he approached the door at an angle, being careful to avoid standing directly in the line of fire. Multiple locks, all state of the art, secured the apartment against intruders. The polished wooden door was reinforced with hidden steel struts.

"Who's there?" he called out.

"It's me, Michael Vaughn," a voice replied through the door. "We need to talk."

A concealed peephole on the wall confirmed that his daughter's boyfriend was indeed standing in the hall outside. Jack scowled. What was Vaughn doing at his apartment? He lowered his gun, but did not put it back in its holster. Just because the man outside looked and sounded like Michael Vaughn was no guarantee of his identity. Jack had been fooled by doubles before. Clones, masks, and voice simulators were an established part of his world.

"What is today's identification code?"

"Coelacanth," his visitor answered promptly.

Jack nodded, satisfied. The APO ID codes were changed randomly every twenty-four hours, as a necessary precaution against imposters. "Apothecary," he replied, to complete the protocol, before unlocking the door and opening it.

Vaughn waited outside, a serious expression on his face. He looked as though he had come straight from the airport after returning from Berlin, barely stopping to stow his bags somewhere. His jacket and slacks were rumpled and stubble carpeted his face, which badly needed a shave. His eyes quickly noted the gun in Jack's hand, then focused squarely on his face. If the sight of the weapon gave him pause, he showed no sign of it. Jack fully expected that Vaughn was armed as well. In fact, he would have been severely disappointed if the younger agent wasn't carrying a gun.

Jack's attitude toward Vaughn had evolved over time. At first, he had disapproved of his daughter's relationship with the man, considering Vaughn to be handicapped by a dangerously naive sense of morality. Life, and a treacherous bitch of a wife, had toughened Vaughn up considerably, however, and Jack had grudgingly come to respect the other man's abilities. There were worse men his daughter could be involved with, especially now that Lauren Reed was dead. If Michael Vaughn made Sydney happy, Jack no longer intended to stand in their way.

None of this meant he was happy to find Vaughn on his doorstep that evening, however.

"How can I help you, Agent Vaughn?" he said frostily, making no move to invite the other man in. It was well after 9:00 P.M., yet Jack suspected that he would be up reading about the alias killings for several hours to come. Vaughn's visit was an unwelcome interruption.

"It's about Sydney," the younger man said. He nodded at the interior of the apartment. "I'd be more comfortable discussing this with you in private."

Making Vaughn comfortable was low on Jack's list of priorities, but he granted that APO business was best discussed away from prying eyes. Bowing to the inevitable, he stepped aside and let Vaughn enter. Jack gritted his teeth as he closed and bolted the door behind them.

He had not been expecting company, so he quickly swept his gaze over the apartment to make certain that all was as it should be. Not that he cared about Vaughn's opinion of his housekeeping, of course, but he still felt somewhat . . . exposed . . . having his personal quarters laid out for the other man's inspection.

The living room was sparsely but tastefully furnished. A black leather sofa and easy chair faced the glass coffee table, which held a small collection of hardcover books beneath it. History, mostly, plus a few serious biographies. More books rested upon the mantel of a built-in brick fireplace. A Persian carpet, obtained during a mission in the Suez some years ago, covered the tile floor. A large-screen TV, which Jack used primarily to keep track of the news, occupied one corner of the apartment. A single framed print hung upon the stark beige walls; it was there only to conceal the peephole he had used a few moments before.

Jack frowned at the "borrowed" documents resting out in plain sight. *No matter,* he assured himself. After Vaughn's recent unauthorized inquiries into his father's death, the headstrong young agent was in no position to criticize Jack for bending the rules. Vaughn was lucky he hadn't been prosecuted after that business in Bordeaux and Darmstadt. *I could have had him put away for that,* Jack thought.

More troubling, on a personal level, were the empty syringe and the plastic pill containers sitting upon the coffee table as well. Jack was still being treated by Dr. Liddell for radiation sickness, and he had been taking his medication when Vaughn arrived. It was irrational, he knew, but it bothered him to have evidence of his physical vulnerability displayed so openly, especially in front of his daughter's lover. *At least I no longer need that damned cane.*

"Thank you for seeing me," Vaughn said, paying little attention to his surroundings. Jack recalled that Vaughn had been here once before, when he and Sydney had searched the apartment for clues to Jack's temporary disappearance several weeks back. The senior agent winced at the memory. That had been a difficult time.

"Well?" He did not bother with pleasantries. "What's so important that you have to disturb me at my home?"

Vaughn took Jack's harsh tone in stride. "I didn't think you would want to have this conversation at the office." He turned to face Sydney's father. "It concerns these so-called alias killings."

"What about them?" Jack asked.

"You can't fool me, Jack." Vaughn remained on his feet, standing just inside the apartment. "I know you're investigating these murders, despite Sloane's orders to the contrary." His eyes met Jack's forbidding gaze. "I want in."

Jack was impressed by the steely resolve in his visitor's voice. He couldn't deny that, like him, Vaughn cared deeply for his daughter. He had proven that on numerous occasions, and had even helped Jack spring Sydney from captivity more than once. Jack could hardly expect him to stand idly by while a nameless killer targeted Sydney, however obliquely. *Vaughn's demonstrated his worth in the past,* he acknowledged. *I would be a fool not to take advantage of his talents.*

He experienced a momentary qualm over diverting Vaughn's energies from the Murnau investigation, but he quickly suppressed it. Sydney's safety took priority.

"Very well," he conceded, adopting a less adversarial tone. He scooped up his medications and hustled them out of sight. "Please take a seat." He hesitated, unaccustomed to playing host. "Er, can I offer you a drink . . . or perhaps some coffee?"

"No, thank you," Vaughn demurred. He sat down on the edge of the leather easy chair. "Maybe later."

"Fine." Jack returned to the couch, intent on getting down to business. "You can speak freely, by the way. This apartment is regularly swept for surveillance equipment. It's one hundred percent clean."

"Why am I not surprised?" Vaughn quipped. He gestured at the files lying open in front of them. "What sort of progress have you made?"

Jack tapped the folders. "At present I'm reviewing SD-6's mission logs, circa 2001, in order to compile a list of viable suspects. Specifically, I'm looking for individuals who may hold a personal grudge against Sydney, who are also likely to know the particulars of her various false identities."

"Sounds promising," Vaughn said. "God knows, plenty of our enemies have managed to get far too close to Sydney in the past." He grimaced at the thought. "What about Sark? Or Allison Doren?"

Jack shook his head. "Sark remains at large, but this isn't his style. He's an opportunist first and foremost; revenge is seldom his primary motivation. Also, if I may speak bluntly, if Sark bears a grudge against anyone in APO, it's against you . . . for executing Lauren Reed." Vaughn's late and unlamented wife had been Julian Sark's secret lover, as well as a double agent working against the CIA. Moreover, Vaughn had brutally interrogated Sark more than once.

And vise versa.

Vaughn's expression darkened, but he did not object to Jack's dragging up such painful memories. "True enough," he said tersely.

"Allison Doren is believed to be dead," Jack continued, "although I'll grant that I take such pronouncements with a grain of salt. For the time being, however, we should probably start with suspects still known to be among the living."

He quickly ran through the other obvious candidates. "Anna Espinosa remains in federal custody. Maya Rao is missing and presumed dead. McKenas Cole is in hiding and cannot be ruled out as a suspect, but he's not known to bear any special enmity against Sydney; Sloane is more his bête noire. Katya Derevko remains in custody, and claims to have Sydney's best interests at heart." Jack paused, uncertain whether to take Katya's claims at face value. The true loyalties of Sydney's duplicitous aunt remained cloudy at best. *I need to have a serious talk with Katya someday.*

"And Elena?"

Jack hesitated before responding. Elena Derevko—Sydney's other, more sinister aunt—was an ongoing source of anxiety for him where both Sydney and Nadia were concerned. Jack knew for a fact that Elena had been covertly spying on her nieces for decades. Furthermore, he was increasingly coming to suspect that Elena was behind many of the byzantine conspiracies bedeviling their lives these days. That brainwashed "clone" of Arvin Sloane, for example. But was she responsible for the alias killings as well?

"I don't know," he confessed. "In my gut, though, I don't think this is Elena. Recent evidence suggests that Elena is pursuing an agenda that hinges on Rambaldi somehow." The prophecies and artifacts of the visionary fifteenth-century seer continued to inspire cults and cabals that threatened the world's security. "I just don't see a Rambaldi connection here."

"Neither do I," Vaughn admitted. He tried another tack. "How about Murnau?"

"A strong possibility." Jack recalled that Sydney had suspected Murnau as well. "Certainly, his reputation suggests that he is vindictive enough to pursue such an elaborate vendetta. The rest of APO's resources are already devoted to his capture, however, so I am inclined to pursue another line of inquiry while working 'off the clock,' as it were."

Vaughn arched an eyebrow. "Such as?"

"Perhaps we need to look even closer to home . . . within SD-6 for example." Jack lifted a folder from the stack of files. "At its height, SD-6 employed dozens of people, including field agents and support staff. After Sydney brought down the Alliance, her captured coworkers were brought in for questioning."

"I remember that," Vaughn said. "I took part in some of those debriefings. It turned out that, like Sydney at first, the vast majority of the staff had been unaware of SD-6's true nature as a terrorist organization. They had truly believed SD-6 to be a legitimate branch of the CIA."

Jack nodded. "Exactly. As a result, they largely escaped criminal prosecution. Some, like Dixon and Marshall, were recruited by the real Agency, while others were allowed to enter the private sector. Most landed on their feet eventually, but there was some collateral damage in the form of suicides, divorces, and ruined careers. It's possible that one of these casualties blames Sydney for 'betraying' SD-6."

"Do you have anybody particular in mind?" Vaughn asked.

Jack removed a photograph from the folder and slid it across the table toward Vaughn. The black-and-white mug shot showed a slender, middle-aged man whose delicate features bordered on the androgynous. Coffee-colored skin bespoke a biracial ancestry. Wire-frame glasses rested upon his nose. Slightly buck teeth could have benefited from a good orthodontist.

"Lewis Fretz," Jack informed Vaughn. "A midlevel staff member formerly employed by SD-6. Fretz's job was to manufacture and document the various fake identities used by Sydney and the other field agents. Unlike the majority of his colleagues, he refused to cooperate with the authorities, who ended up making an example of him. He spent some time in a federal prison before dropping off the map several months ago."

In truth, Jack barely remembered Fretz. He had just been an anonymous cog in the insidious machine that was SD-6. That the man's life had been sent into a tailspin by the downfall of SD-6 had also largely escaped Jack's notice . . . until now.

Could Lewis Fretz be the alias killer?

Vaughn inspected the mug shot. "This is the guy who furnished Sydney with her fake IDs back then?" The implications of Fretz's former occupation were not lost on him. "That gives him both the means *and* the motive." He slid the photo back over to Jack. "So where is he hiding these days?"

"That's what we need to find out."

CHAPTER 5

SANTA MONICA BOULEVARD
WEST HOLLYWOOD

Thursday night and the boulevard was hopping. Clubbers, natives, and tourists roamed the busy sidewalks, beneath the lambent glow of the street-lights. The sun was just setting, but the district's vibrant nightlife was already under way. Music blared from the open windows of the cars slowly cruising down the tree-lined thoroughfare. Hip, stylishly dressed people poured in and out of the clubs, coffee houses, and art galleries facing the street. Others lounged at sidewalk cafés, taking in the scene while sipping their drinks. Laughter and the tinkling of glassware added to the hubbub. A smoggy haze shimmered in the twilight.

Not bad for a weeknight, Nadia thought as she strode down the sidewalk. The zesty atmosphere reminded her of her native Buenos Aires. A pair of handsome, well-groomed men walked hand in hand in front of her; this stretch of West Hollywood was the heart of the city's gay and lesbian community. *I guess it's fitting, then, that I'm here tailing another woman.*

Vicky King, to be exact. The spiky-haired redhead was a few yards ahead of Nadia, oblivious to the other woman's discreet surveillance. She was also presumably unaware that her life was in imminent danger.

Close analysis of the earlier murders had revealed that the victims were being killed in chronological order, matching the sequence in which Sydney had first used their names as aliases. This pattern suggested that the next target would be a woman named Victoria King, an alias Sydney had once employed while posing as the daughter of a wealthy industrialist on a private resort island off the coast of Kenya. That was before Nadia's time, of course, but she had carefully reviewed the file on that assignment.

Although there were several Victoria (and Vicky) Kings living in and around Los Angeles, only the woman walking ahead of Nadia matched Sydney's approximate age and description. Frankly, Nadia didn't think that the redhead, who was decked out in black leather trousers and a matching vest, looked that much like her sister, but she was the right age and build. That was enough to make her the most likely target, at least in theory.

I just hope to God we've got the right Victoria, Nadia thought anxiously. She shadowed the other woman, being careful to keep two or three people between them. The crowded sidewalk made it easy to follow Vicky unobserved, but it also hid from Nadia the intentions of a possible stalker. Nadia worriedly scanned the faces of the people around her, all too aware that any one of them could be the alias killer. She felt the weight of the solemn responsibility laid upon her. *It's up to Weiss and me to keep Vicky King alive.*

She decided to check in with her partner. "Evergreen to Houdini," she subvocalized into her communicator as she held a Nokia cell phone up to her lips to disguise her actions. "Can you read me?"

"Right behind you, babe." Weiss's cheery tone

brought a smile to her lips. Glancing back over her shoulder, she glimpsed a red Ford Focus gliding down the street behind her. Heavy traffic slowed the Ford's progress, keeping it in view. Weiss winked at her from behind the wheel. "Have I mentioned how smoking you look in that outfit?"

Neither she nor Weiss had ever worked for SD-6, so they were unlikely to be recognized by the killer, but she had disguised her appearance anyway, just to play it safe. A green velvet bustier matched her call sign. Her tight jeans were tucked into chocolate suede boots. An ocean of hair gel had lacquered her dark tresses to her scalp, turning her hair into a tight, pixielike cap. A phony gold piercing adorned her lower lip. Dark smudges of black makeup gave her raccoon eyes.

On any other street her getup might have attracted attention, but here she just blended into the crowd. That was the idea. She wasn't trying to vamp anyone tonight, only to keep a close eye on Vicky.

"Keep your mind on the mission," she teased him. They had been dating for a while now. Whether it was serious remained to be seen. "Tonight you're my backup, not my boyfriend."

"Whatever." He flirted with her over the comms. "All I'm saying is, that look definitely works for you. Maybe you can hang on to that out-fit after the mission?"

"Oh, so you're already bored with the usual me?" Resisting the temptation to sneak a peek at his expression, she grinned as she put him on the spot. But before she could find out how he intended to extricate himself from her trap, she saw Vicky King slow to a halt up ahead. "Hang on," she reported, immediately back to business. "We may have reached our destination."

Farther down the sidewalk Vicky joined the line outside a shadowy doorway tucked between an art gallery and a gay bookstore. A narrow alley sepa-rated the buildings. Two butch-looking women guarded the threshold, which appeared to lead to a nightclub located above the gallery. A purple neon sign bore the club's name: MYTHOS. Flashing strobe lights could be seen through the second-story win-dows. EVERY THURSDAY—LADIES' NIGHT! proclaimed bright paper fliers plastered all around the doorway. Sure enough, Nadia observed that the line was 100 percent female.

Good thing I'm the one doing the tailing tonight.

"Looks like she's going in." Nadia took a place in the line about five heads behind her unknowing charge. Nearby a group of smokers mingled on the sidewalk, driven into the street by the city's smoking ban. Nadia fanned the noxious fumes away from her. "I guess I'm hitting a club."

"Well, don't have too much fun," Weiss warned her. "Just remember what team you're playing for." The red Focus continued down the street, past Mythos. "I'll keep circling the block. Who knows? Maybe I'll luck out and find a parking spot close by."

"Copy that, Houdini." She tucked the cell phone back into her rear pocket. A few feet away the women at the door greeted Vicky warmly. Nadia guessed that she was a regular. Was the alias killer aware of that? If so, the assassin could very well be waiting inside.

All the more reason not to let her out of my sight, Nadia thought. She nervously watched Vicky disappear into the building. Unhappy at losing sight of the other woman, if only for a moment, Nadia waited impatiently in the line, even as the queue rapidly carried her forward. As she neared the door, however, she spotted one of the doorkeepers running a handheld security wand along the outline of the latest arrival. The latex-clad club hopper presented a cell phone and a PDA for the doorkeeper's inspection before being waved inside. The female watchdog then used the metal detector to search the next woman in line.

Nadia instantly remembered the Beretta in her handbag. "Hold my place, will you?" she asked the woman behind her as she exited the line long enough to run over to a nearby recycling bin. She discreetly deposited the handgun into the blue plastic container, while making a mental note to retrieve it later. "Thanks!" she said breathlessly as she hurried back to her place in the line. "Had to ditch some leftover aluminum foil from lunch."

Minutes ticked by before she finally reached the front of the line. After the metal detector found nothing amiss, she quickly paid the cover charge. A rubber stamp left an inky impression of the Venus de Milo on the back of her hand. "So you can go in and out," the bouncer explained. "Welcome to Mythos. Have fun!"

"Count on it!" Nadia glanced briefly at the hand stamp. *Not a bad way to pass coded messages,* she thought, filing the idea away for future reference. The doorway led to a narrow flight of stairs, and she hurried up the steps to the second floor, anxious to locate Vicky King before the killer could. Finally she entered the club through a door on the landing.

Loud music and flashing lights immediately assaulted her senses. Mythos was packed, and the crush of bodies was enough to raise the temperature inside the club to a near tropical degree of sultriness. Thirsty patrons flocked to the polished mahogany bar running along the rear of the space, while dozens of partying women gyrated on the dance floor, beneath the frenzied strobe lights. Colored filters cast polychromatic shadows upon the glistening faces of the sweaty dancers. Mounted television sets, with the sound turned down, ran clips from *The Hunger* and *Dracula's Daughter* on a continuous loop. Throbbing techno music drowned out the din of umpteen conversations. The eclectic attire ran from serious fetish wear to cool and casual, and everything else in between. A pair of glamorous lipstick lesbians made out in a shadowy nook, only a few feet away from Nadia. Neither one of them looked like Vicky King.

Ignoring the amorous couple, Nadia desperately scanned the scene, searching for Vicky. "Excuse me," she murmured as she forced her way through the throng, trying to get a better view of the dance floor. Each passing second upped the strain on her nerves. What if the alias killer had already stolen Vicky away, luring her off to her doom? There was no reason why the murderer couldn't be a woman; Nadia herself had killed more than few people. As a Derevko, murder was practically in her blood.

Please let me find her, Nadia prayed. Besides Vicky, her sister was depending on her as well. She couldn't face the prospect of telling Sydney that another of her namesakes had been killed. *I can't imagine what she's going through right now.*

A sea of unfamiliar faces surrounded her. Nadia grimly considered the possibility of never locating Vicky amid the disorienting strobe lights. Then, just as she was about to confess to Weiss that she had lost their charge, she spotted the redhead on the dance floor, grinding enthusiastically amid a knot of dancing women. Her arms above her head, she swayed to the beat of the percussive, electronic music.

Nadia let out a sigh of relief. Not only was

Vicky still alive and well, but she seemed to be having the time of her life. *Good for her,* Nadia thought. She envied the other woman's carefree spirit. Vicky King didn't have to watch the crowd for lurking assassins. *That's my job.* Still, maybe nothing would happen tonight. If they were lucky, Vicky would simply dance the night away without incident. *I can live with that. As long as no other Victorias die in the meantime.*

Keeping one eye on her spiky-haired target, Nadia migrated to the bar, where she commandeered a stool overlooking the dance floor. She ordered a glass of soda on the rocks, then settled in to watch over Vicky. Although she felt better now that she knew where the woman was, she couldn't afford to relax too much; the bustling dance club was a less than ideal environment in which to play bodyguard to the unsuspecting redhead. Nadia flinched inside every time a stranger came near Vicky. Any one of the surrounding women could be the alias killer, or some accomplice working on the killer's behalf. *For all we know,* she mused, *there could be multiple killers.*

According to a sign over the bar, last call would be at midnight. Nadia just had to keep

Vicky alive until then, and then see her safely back to her apartment in Century City. Unless, of course, Vicky ended up going home with someone. That would complicate matters considerably, especially if that someone was a potential killer. *I guess we'll cross that bridge when we come to it,* Nadia thought.

She took a moment to check all available entrances and escape routes. Besides the door by the stairs, a sign that read FIRE EXIT glowed above a black velvet curtain at the opposite end of the bar. Large glass windows faced the boulevard below, but Nadia wasn't worried about the possibility of a sniper positioned across the street. Not even the best marksman in the world could pick Vicky out of this mob scene, and certainly not at a distance. Plus, the rockin' redhead was nowhere near the windows.

Of course, there was no way to guarantee that Vicky would be safe once she was back home, or at work tomorrow afternoon. Not for the first time, Nadia wished there were more agents assigned to this operation. With just her and Weiss, there was no way they could shadow Vicky King 24/7. But her father had been adamant about not diverting any more resources from the search for Oskar Murnau. Nadia understood his reasoning. But that didn't make Vicky any safer.

On the dance floor a bald woman crept up on Vicky from behind. A bikini top and Bermuda shorts showed off the woman's extensively tattooed torso. Nadia's pulse sped up. Her entire body tensed for action. Was this it? According to the coroner's reports on the first four victims, Kate Jones, Molly Zerdin, Christina Auriti, and Christiana Stephens had each been killed by a single knife thrust to their vital organs. Nadia squinted, trying to catch a glimpse of the newcomer's hands, but the strobe lights and dancing bodies made it impossible to tell if the bald woman had a knife.

Nadia's mouth went dry. What if she was already too late? She hopped off the stool and drew back her glass, ready to hurl it like a missile if necessary. Was Vicky King about to be murdered right before her eyes?

The stranger tapped Vicky on the shoulder. She spun around in surprise. Her eyes widened . . . and a huge smile broke out over her face. Squealing in delight, she hugged the bald woman like she hadn't seen her in years.

Nadia relaxed. It was a false alarm; obviously, the stranger was an old friend of Vicky's. Nadia lowered her glass and let some of the tension drain out of her system. She glanced back at her stool, only to discover that someone had already claimed her seat. Oh, well. She shrugged her shoulders and took a sip of soda. Nadia slowly worked her way toward the dance floor, the better to keep Vicky, who was now dancing with the bald woman, in sight. She suspected she had a long night ahead. Sweat trickled down her bare back. The overheated nightclub felt like a sauna.

Now I understand where the phrase "disco inferno" came from.

An attractive Latina stepped in front of her, blocking her view. Her wavy black hair resembled Nadia's usual style. An off-the-shoulder red satin shift and glittering disco belt enclosed her generous curves. "Hey, gorgeous! Wanna dance?"

"No, thank you," Nadia answered, shouting to be heard over the pounding music. She shifted position to see around the overly friendly woman. "Maybe later."

"My name's Yolanda," the woman volunteered. Her gaze swept over Nadia's body. She obviously liked what she saw. "I've never seen you here before. New in town?"

Nadia groaned inside. *First Weiss, now this chick,* she thought. *Just my luck—I'm irresistible tonight.* "Sort of," she said vaguely, trying not to encourage Yolanda. The last thing she needed right now was someone hitting on her while she was trying to keep tabs on Vicky King. *I wonder how Sydney would handle this situation?*

"Cool," Yolanda said, not giving up. "I'm from Seattle originally." She stepped closer, once again coming between Nadia and her view of the dance floor. Nadia could smell the woman's heavy floral perfume. "What did you say your name was?"

I didn't, Nadia thought. *That's classified information.*

"Back off, lady!" a husky voice intervened as someone draped a possessive arm around Nadia's shoulders. "She's taken."

Caught off guard, Nadia turned to see Sydney standing beside her, glaring balefully at Yolanda. A Cher-length white wig fell past her shoulders, and green contact lenses made her harder to recognize. A midriff-baring black sequined top and a tiny black miniskirt lured attention away from her face.

Cubic zirconium glittered in her navel, and her zebra-striped boots were planted firmly on the floor.

Yolanda got the message. "Sorry. Didn't mean to butt in." She backed away and, within minutes, was chatting up a blonde femme over by the bar. Nadia wondered for a second if she should be offended.

"Thanks," she said. She looked at her sister in confusion. "Not that I don't appreciate the timely save, but what are you doing here? Aren't you supposed to be chasing Murnau?"

Sydney's somber expression showed through her disguise. "I just couldn't stay away, not while another one of my 'namesakes' is in danger." She shrugged her shoulders. "I figured another pair of eyes couldn't hurt."

I suppose, Nadia thought. She didn't know whether to be grateful for Sydney's assistance, or annoyed that her sister didn't trust her to protect Vicky on her own. Maybe a little bit of both. She wrapped her arm around Sydney's waist, so as to discourage any unwanted admirers. "You realize, of course, that this whole 'girlfriends' routine is kind of icky, given that you're my sister and all."

"You want icky?" Sydney whispered back. "Try convincing your own father that you're actually his wife." Sydney had needed to do just that a few weeks back, when Jack's recent illness had rendered him delusional. "*That* will keep you in therapy for a while."

Good point, Nadia thought.

On the dance floor Vicky King remained oblivious to their attention. Nadia was impressed by her stamina; the energetic redhead looked like she was ready to dance all night. Nadia decided it was a good thing that Sydney was there. At least they could cover for each other from time to time. She gulped down the last of her soda. *I'm going to need a bathroom break at some point.*

"Evergreen to Houdini." Nadia began, wanting to make sure Weiss was aware of Sydney's arrival on the scene, but then she worried about who might be monitoring her transmissions back at APO. She hoped Sydney wouldn't get in hot water for disobeying Sloane's directives. But then again, Weiss had to know about the additional manpower. "Phoenix is here to provide support."

"So I hear, Evergreen," Weiss replied. His masculine voice sounded strangely out of place among all the female conversations around her. "Guess you're having a real girls' night out."

Sydney cupped a hand over her own ear. Nadia guessed that she was listening in. *That's probably how she found us in the first place.*

"I'll keep you posted," she promised Weiss. Before she could sign off, however, a booming voice called out loudly from behind the bar.

"Is there a Sydney Bristow here?" the bartender shouted over the clamor. She held up a flashing cell phone. "Call for Sydney Bristow!"

What the hell? Sydney thought.

She exchanged a puzzled look with Nadia. Nobody, not even APO, knew that she was here tonight. She hadn't even told her father about her plans. Her decision to covertly join this operation had been a last-minute impulse.

"Sydney Bristow?"

Now what do I do? Sydney hesitated, but curiosity got the better of her. "Here I am!" she called back to the bartender and began elbowing her way over to the bar, earning herself a few muttered protests and curious glances along the way. "Coming through!" Nadia followed closely in her wake, holding on to her sister's hand. Sydney disliked attracting so much attention, especially with her real name being bandied about, but she saw no alternative if she wanted to find out who was trying to contact her this way. "Hang on!"

Reaching the bar, she accepted the phone from the bartender, who looked mildly annoyed at having to take a personal call for a customer she didn't even know. Sydney ignored the bartender's dirty look and spoke into the phone. "Hello? Who is this?"

An unfamiliar voice whispered into her ear. "Hi there, Sydney. About time you showed up. I've been trying to get your attention for weeks now."

A chill ran down Sydney's spine as she realized she was speaking to the killer. "Next time just send me an e-mail," she said angrily. "You didn't have to kill all those women."

"An e-mail? How impersonal would that have been!" The mocking voice sounded female. "Nice of you to finally join the party. What a shame you're already too late!"

What? Sydney suddenly realized that she heard music playing in the background on the other end of the line, the same synthetic techno that was rocking the club at this very minute. *She's here!*

Sydney spun around and urgently searched the crowded club for the killer. She lurched up onto her toes to try to see over the heads of the cavorting women surrounding her. "Vicky!" she yelled at Nadia. "Get to Vicky . . . now!"

Fear gripped Sydney's heart as her eyes zeroed in on the carefree redhead. To her dismay, she saw a tall, dark-skinned woman swiftly approach Vicky from behind. The stranger was dressed like a biker chick, complete with a fringed black leather jacket, chaps, and chain hat, and she held a sleek silver cell phone up to her lips. Leather riding gloves protected the phone from her fingerprints. A quartz blade glittered in her other hand.

"Say good-bye to Victoria," the killer taunted Sydney.

"No!" Sydney shouted helplessly. She plunged into the crowd after Nadia, but the dense wall of bodies obstructed them both. Sydney could only watch in horror as the killer came up behind Vicky and drove the crystalline knife deep into her midsection. She twisted the knife to inflict maximum damage. The redhead's body stiffened in shock and her mouth fell open. The edge of the blade gleamed wetly as the killer withdrew the knife in an instant. The razor-sharp quartz, Sydney realized, was perfect for evading metal detectors.

The killer had planned out the murder down to the last detail.

So deftly was the deed done that the rest of the dancers didn't even realize what had happened until Vicky collapsed onto the dance floor. Blood soaked through her leather vest, and beneath the colored lights the crimson fluid looked black as pitch. The bald woman let out a bloodcurdling scream.

Chaos erupted inside Mythos. Panicked women fled the dance floor, trampling over one another in their frantic desire to escape the site of the murder. Shouts and sobs competed with the raucous dance beats until someone finally had the presence of mind to turn the music off. The spinning strobe lights gave the frenzied exodus an eerie, slow-motion quality, like a trip through a haunted house on Halloween. Discarded glasses crunched beneath racing high heels and boots. People slipped and fell on spilled drinks and ice.

By now, the killer was halfway to the fire exit. "You see to Vicky," Sydney yelled at Nadia as she took off after the murderous biker chick. Terrified clubbers rushing in the opposite direction slowed Sydney down; she felt like a salmon fighting its way upstream. She reached instinctively for her gun, then remembered that she had ditched it before facing the metal detector downstairs. *Probably just as well,* she realized. She could hardly fire into the fleeing mob. There had already been one civilian casualty. "Out of the way!" she shouted. "Let me through!"

The killer wasn't the only woman dashing for the exit. A bottleneck formed beneath the illuminated sign, blocking the killer's escape. Frightened clubgoers formed a clot in the doorway, pushing and shoving their way past the black velvet curtain. The killer turned to see Sydney gaining on her. They were maybe seven feet apart, tops.

Their eyes met through the tangle of women between them. The murderer's dark brown eyes glared at Sydney. The brim of the killer's hat threw the upper half of her face into shadow, but Sydney was fairly sure she had never seen the other woman before. Her coffee-hued complexion hinted at Arab or Indian roots. A malicious smile lifted the assassin's lips.

"There!" she cried out. The killer pointed an accusing finger at Sydney. Her voice quavered and a look of faux terror came over her face. "She's the one! She stabbed that girl!"

Multiple pairs of eyes turned toward Sydney. She saw both fear and anger in the faces of the women around her. The women nearest her pulled away fearfully, but a few of the braver women clenched their fists and sized Sydney up with their eyes. Among them was the bald woman who had been dancing with Vicky right before she was murdered. Hatred contorted the woman's tearstained face, and a tattooed dragon writhed upon her quaking torso.

"Get her!" the bald woman shouted angrily. She pointed a shaking finger at Sydney. "Don't let her get away!"

"No . . . wait!" Sydney protested. "You've got the wrong wom—"

The bald woman and three of her friends charged at Sydney from all directions. Sydney quickly assessed the situation. She didn't want to hurt these women. She couldn't blame them for their anger, however misplaced. Her best bet was to make a quick example of the bravest would-be vigilantes. . . .

Krav Maga training kicked in as Sydney fluidly moved from defense to attack and back again. An elbow jab caught the bald ringleader in the stomach, causing her to double over, gasping. A second later she grabbed onto a second woman with both hands and swung her into a third woman who was coming at her with an upraised beer bottle. The nameless women crashed to the floor in a tangle of aching limbs and groans. A fourth woman tried to sneak up on her from behind, but Sydney spotted her in the mirror above the bar. A rear defensive kick sent the woman tumbling backward into a throng of hysterical club hoppers.

The Israelis called Sydney's brand of fighting *retzev*, a Hebrew word meaning "continuous motion." The idea was to train your body to react automatically in combat situations, so that one strike flowed continuously into the next without conscious thought. In any case, it was more than a handful of half-terrified night club visitors were prepared to cope with. By now, the bald woman had recovered enough to throw a punch at Sydney's jaw, but the disguised agent expertly ducked beneath the blow. She came in fast past the other woman's defenses to deliver a solid uppercut to her opponent's chin. The tattooed woman toppled backward onto the floor, her dragon heaving. Shocked gasps arose from the crowd.

Sydney cracked her knuckles. She'd had tougher workouts sparring with Vaughn.

She looked around to see if anyone else wanted to take a crack at her, but the brutally effective way she had dealt with her first few attackers seemed to have put more than enough fear into the hearts of the remaining women. Spooked bystanders cleared out of her way, joining the rush for the stairs across the room. Sydney was relieved that she didn't have to take on the entire crowd; there was only one woman she wanted to take down right now: the monster who had just killed Vicky King.

But where was the assassin now? Peering ahead, Sydney saw that her enemy had taken advantage of the brawl to reach the black velvet curtain beneath the exit sign. The hanging fabric flapped behind the killer as she slipped past the curtain and out of sight.

Not so fast, Sydney thought. Jumping over the groaning bodies at her feet, she sprinted over to the curtain and yanked it aside, ready to defend herself if the killer was waiting on the other side of the drapes. Instead, she saw a gray metal door swing shut directly ahead of her. Sydney kicked it back open and stepped out onto a fire escape overlooking the alley below. The killer stood poised at the opposite end of the wrought-iron scaffolding. A decel cable was wrapped loosely around her waist.

"Hold it!" Sydney shouted. She lunged for the killer, but, before she could grab on to the other woman, the biker chick had jumped clear of the fire escape. Holding on to the cable, which she must have set up in advance, she rappelled down the side of the building onto the floor of the alley below. A Harley-Davidson motorcycle was waiting for her. She jumped onto the bike and hit the ignition. The roar of a powerful V-twin engine disturbed the night. The killer grinned up at Sydney and gave her the finger before burning rubber out of the alley.

Sydney swore under her breath and gripped the iron guardrail in frustration. From two stories up, she watched the chopper zoom out of sight, turning right onto Santa Monica Boulevard. There was no way she could catch up with the killer now.

But maybe someone else could.

"Phoenix to Houdini!" she shouted into her comms. "The killer is on the move. She's making a run for it!"

CHAPTER 6

SANTA MONICA BOULEVARD

Weiss had circled the block several times before he finally found a parking spot within sight of Mythos. He leaned back against the driver's seat as he watched the line winding its way into the hot night-club. So far he hadn't spied anything or anyone suspicious, but then again, he had absolutely no idea what to watch out for. Somehow he doubted that the alias killer was going to have a hit list tattooed on his or her forehead.

Although, that would certainly make this mission easier, he thought wryly.

Weiss was prepared for a long stakeout. An open bag of pretzels sat on the passenger seat next to him, while a two-liter bottle of Coke rested on the floor, guaranteeing him an ample supply of caffeine throughout the evening. Along with the Colt automatic holstered under his jacket, he was also armed with about fifty dollars' worth of quarters to feed into the parking meter.

Never let it be said that I don't plan ahead.

An amateur magician, as noted by his call sign, he shuffled a deck of cards as he wondered how Nadia and Sydney were faring inside Mythos. Truth be told, the prospect of his girlfriend and her sister infiltrating ladies' night at a gay nightclub was nearly as provocative as it was unsettling, and part of him wished he could be a fly on the wall. Too bad neither of the women were wired for video. . . .

On a professional level, he found himself torn when it came to imagining an outcome for tonight's mission. On the one hand, he hoped that the evening would remain uneventful and that Vicky King would be spared any close brushes with death. On the other hand, if the killer didn't come after Vicky tonight, then the whole exercise would be a waste and they would be no closer to tracking down the assassin than before. Unless the killer made a move, he and Nadia (and Sydney) would be right back at square one, with the murderer still on the loose.

Weiss shook his head. He and Sydney had been friends for years now; he knew how much this senseless killing spree had to be eating her up inside. He couldn't blame Syd for horning in on tonight's operation. He'd probably do the same if he were in her shoes.

"Call for Sydney Bristow!"

He sat up straight as, over the comms, he heard a loud feminine voice paging Sydney inside the club. What was going on? He listened intently, his playing cards frozen in midshuffle. Moments later high-pitched shouts and screams rang out in the background. He could hear sheer terror in the women's voices. Adrenaline rushed through his system as he realized that something had taken a serious turn for the worse.

"Evergreen! What's happening over there? What is your status?"

"We have a situation!" Nadia reported tersely. She sounded too busy to explain in detail. "Hold your position!"

"Copy that, Evergreen!"

He hastily merged the playing cards into a single deck, then thrust them back into his pocket. His hands gripped the steering wheel as he peered anxiously out the windshield at the club across the street. A stream of panic-stricken women came rushing out of Mythos's ground-floor entrance, spilling out onto the sidewalk. Many of them kept on running, trying to put as much distance between themselves and the nightclub as possible. The line to get into the club rapidly dispersed as word spread of whatever atrocity had taken place upstairs. Distraught escapees shouted for the police, while dozens of other shaken clubbers put their cell phones to work, dialing 911. Over the comms, Weiss heard a fight break out inside Mythos. Shrieks and groans accompanied the sound of bodies hitting the floor.

He squirmed restlessly in his seat. This was the worst part of providing backup on a mission: listening from a distance while your colleagues faced genuine peril. He was tempted to abandon the Ford and rush to his fellow agents' assistance, but he dutifully stayed inside the car as instructed, just in case the girls needed to make a hasty getaway.

Starting the engine, he buckled his seat belt and waited for Syd or Nadia to update him, all the while trying to make sense of the violent noises coming over the comms.

At least he hadn't heard any gunshots.

"Phoenix to Houdini!" Sydney's voice barked into his ear. "The killer is on the move. She's making a run for it!"

Almost simultaneously a motorcycle came charging out of the alley beside Mythos. Weiss glimpsed a leather-clad woman aboard the chopper. "The chick on the bike?" he asked urgently.

"That's her!" Sydney confirmed. "Don't let her get away!"

"I'm on it!" Throwing the Ford into drive, he pulled out into traffic. Squealing brakes and blaring horns greeted his sudden entry onto the boulevard. The commotion attracted the attention of the mystery biker, who glanced back over her shoulder at the noise. She spied the bright red coupe closing in on her, and sped up in response. The metallic blue Harley-Davidson zoomed ahead, weaving recklessly through the cars in front of her. Her hat blew off her head, freeing her glossy black tresses to stream behind her in the wind.

Weiss wasn't about to let the killer give him the slip. Thanks to Marshall, the Ford came complete with a couple of very nonstandard options. Weiss pushed a button on the dashboard and a spinning red light rose from the roof of the car as an ear-piercing police siren demanded that all other cars get out of his way. It occurred to Weiss that even the Ford had an alias. Right now it was doing a very convincing job of impersonating a police car.

The heavy traffic parted before him and he hit the gas, staying in hot pursuit of the fleeing motor-cycle. The biker opened up the throttle, hitting more than eighty miles an hour. Weiss floored it as well. Pretzels flew across the passenger seat, and the overturned Coke bottle rolled back and forth across the floor of the car.

Weiss kept both hands on the wheel. He decided to keep his pistol in its holster for now; he was unlikely to hit a moving target while firing left-handed from the driver's side window. Instead, he concentrated on matching the motor-cycle's speed, while trying not to lose control of the car. He didn't care if he had to chase the killer all the way to the border. The bike had to run out of gas eventually, right?

Give it all you've got, babe. My tank's bigger than yours.

The Harley roared through a yellow light at the intersection of Fairfax and Santa Monica. Only four car lengths behind the bike, Weiss honked loudly on his horn as he ran the red light. Cars and trucks slammed on their brakes to let the Ford rocket through. Weiss breathed a sigh of relief as he passed through the intersection without a scratch. Spotting a green light ahead, he accelerated to nearly a hundred miles an hour, only to see a careless jaywalker dart in front of him. The man wore a green velour jogging suit and his head bobbed in rhythm to the tune playing over his iPod.

"Watch out, you idiot!" Weiss blurted out, but the jogger was caught up in his musical soundscape. Weiss tugged hard on the wheel, veering left just in time to avoid turning the oblivious dude into road pizza. The Ford swerved across two lanes of traffic before straightening out and resuming its pursuit of the Harley. Weiss wiped a few nervous beads of perspiration from his brow. *That was close!*

He heard real police sirens behind him. The high-speed chase had brought out the local constabulary.

Glancing in his rearview mirror, Weiss saw at least four black-and-white police vehicles chasing after him, apparently not convinced by his counterfeit red light and siren. Hearing the distinctive whirring of helicopter blades, he spotted a TV news helicopter swooping down from the sky behind him. *Great,* he thought sarcastically. *I just became a special news report.* He had no doubt that his breakneck pursuit of the motorcycle was being aired live all over Los Angeles, if not nationally. *Hayden Chase and her people are going to have their hands full covering this up afterward.*

Weiss couldn't worry about that at the moment. All that mattered was catching the biker and putting a stop to the alias killings. Was Vicky King still alive? There hadn't been time to find out yet, but he feared the worst. Ignoring the cops and copters behind him, he remained focused on the woman on the speeding motorcycle. Plummer Park whizzed by on his left, but he barely noticed the greenery. His jaw was set in determination. Sydney was counting on him, and he owed it to her to make sure that no more of her namesakes were murdered.

Flashing red lights glowed up ahead, and Weiss saw that the LAPD had set up a roadblock.

Black-and-white police cars were lined up across the boulevard, while armed officers took up defensive positions behind the makeshift barricade. They looked like they weren't buying the Ford's alias either. "Terrific," Weiss muttered, wondering if it was too late to switch to the Murnau assignment instead. Hunting for an international terrorist with the formula for an experimental superexplosive was starting to sound like a breeze in comparison. *My mother didn't raise me to star in a remake of* Smokey and the Bandit.

The roadblock was right in front of the oncoming motorcycle. Weiss hoped that the biker would do the sensible thing and surrender, but that wasn't in the cards; at the last minute, the Harley took a sharp turn to the right and drove up onto the sidewalk, bypassing the cars lined up on the boulevard. Startled cops dove for safety as the bike roared down the sidewalk. The biker leaned forward, pulling a nose wheelie as the Harley's back wheel lifted off the pavement. The slick maneuver turned the rear of the bike into a barrier between the rider and any police bullets. The bike was balanced perfectly on its front wheel, not showing any signs of slowing down.

Oh, hell. Weiss knew what he had to do. Following the biker's lead, he took the Ford onto the sidewalk as well, narrowly missing both a palm tree and a nearby parking meter. A jolt went through his spine as the car took the curb, and he yanked the wheel to the left to avoid plowing through the plate-glass window of an exotic lingerie shop. Sparks flew where the passenger side of the Ford scraped against a fire hydrant. Thankfully, the cops had already cleared the area of pedestrians, but the tables and chairs of a sidewalk café weren't so lucky. The wrought-iron furniture bounced off the Ford's front fender, tablecloths and candleholders went flying, and a painted black stool crunched beneath the car's tires.

Furious cops shouted at him to stop, then took aim at the heedless vehicle. Gunshots popped like firecrackers, making Weiss grateful for the Ford's bulletproof glass and concealed armor plating. Hot lead ricocheted off the rear of the coupe, and muzzle flashes lit up the rearview mirror.

None of the police officers' wild shots tagged the rider on the Harley-Davidson. Once she was past the barricade, the biker swerved back onto the road. Hot on its tail, the Ford flew off the sidewalk, launching off from the curb before touching down on the boulevard. Only Weiss's seat belt kept him from smacking his head against the ceiling. The Ford's shock absorbers were getting a real workout tonight. *Remind me not to open that Coke bottle anytime soon,* he thought. At this point, the shaken-up soda was probably ready to blow like Vesuvius.

Behind him, the cops scrambled to turn their cars around, but Weiss and his fuel-injected quarry had left them temporarily in the dust. Only the scoop-hungry news copter was keeping up with the chase as the blue motorcycle continued to head east on Santa Monica, passing the Hollywood Forever Cemetery on the right. Weiss guessed that the biker was heading for the freeway entrance, several blocks ahead. Was the killer planning to go north into the hills or deeper into downtown Los Angeles? *It doesn't matter,* he thought grimly. *I'm sticking to her like Brad on Angelina.*

"Phoenix to Houdini," Sydney said. The comms made it sound like she was practically sitting in the passenger seat beside him. "What's your status?"

"I'm still in pursuit of the target." He quickly

updated her on his present location and direction. "She's not slowing down, but neither am I." He paused, almost afraid to ask the obvious question. "Er, what's the story there?"

"Vicky King is dead," Syd said bluntly. Her voice was hoarse with emotion, but it didn't quaver. "A single knife-thrust to the heart, just like the others."

"Damn it." Weiss's heart sank, even though he had been half-expecting this news ever since he'd heard the screams coming from inside Mythos. Another innocent person had been killed. He didn't know Vicky King, and he had only seen her from a distance, but he knew she didn't deserve to die like this. "Syd, I'm so sorry. . . ."

"Just get her," she said. Her voice took on a harder edge. "Don't let her get away with this . . . again."

Weiss recognized the icy fury in her tone. It was the same voice she often used when dealing with Arvin Sloane. "Don't worry," he promised. "I'm not going to lose her."

The freeway entrance was less than a mile away. Green metal signs alerted drivers to the junction of Route 101. Weiss kept his gaze fixed on the zooming motorcycle, watching to see which entrance the biker took. He was ready to follow her wherever she went.

Then, to his surprise, the Harley made a tight left turn, leaning so far over that for a moment the rider was only inches above the blacktop and headed the wrong way up the off-ramp.

Weiss's jaw dropped open. DO NOT ENTER signs guarded the freeway exit, but the Harley zipped right past them, clinging to the outer shoulder of the ramp in order to avoid colliding head-on with the trucks and cars leaving the freeway. Terrified drivers honked their horns and swerved away from the oncoming motorcycle while Weiss looked on, aghast.

I'm screwed, he realized. The Harley was small enough to pull off a daredevil stunt like that, but there was no way he could drive the Ford up the off-ramp and onto the freeway without causing a multicar pileup—and God knows how many civilian casualties. Frustrated, Weiss had no choice but to drive past the exit and let the killer make her escape. There wasn't even any point in trying to find the on-ramp; the Harley would be speeding against the flow of the traffic.

Might as well admit it, he thought. *She got away. Again.*

Sirens approached from behind, and he realized that the LAPD had caught up with him. Sighing, he slowed down and looked for a good place to pull over. Removing his Colt from its holster, he tossed it under the passenger seat to avoid any potential unpleasantness. The last thing he needed right now was to get gunned down by a trigger-happy cop. Coming to a stop along the side of the boulevard, Weiss wondered how long it would take the CIA to spring him from police custody. He switched off the Ford's bogus lights and siren. Why provoke the cops more than he already had?

Dealing with an irate police force was the least of his worries, however. As he stepped out of the car, with his hands raised above his head, a more important problem weighed heavily on his mind.

How am I going to tell Sydney that the alias killer is still on the loose?

CHAPTER 7

APO BUNKER

Sloane was not amused.

"I am greatly disappointed, Agent Bristow, to discover that you were working on another case instead of tracking Oskar Murnau. I assigned you to the Murnau matter with good reason, and I do not appreciate your moonlighting behind my back."

He stood stiffly behind his desk as he confronted Sydney in the privacy of his office. Her report on the previous night's events was open in front of him, along with copies of the morning papers. Weiss's high-speed chase through West Hollywood was front-page news, as was the murder at the nightclub. A headline—GOOD SAMARITAN PURSUES LADIES' NIGHT KILLER—presented the CIA's spin on the night's activities. SUSPECTED MURDERER EVADES CAPTURE.

"I was on my own time," Sydney replied, unfazed by Sloane's disapproving gaze. She couldn't care less about what Sloane thought of her, and she wasn't about to apologize for trying to catch the alias killer. Her only regret was that her intervention had failed to save Vicky King's life. "What I do in my off-hours is my own concern."

"Yours is hardly a nine-to-five job, Sydney, and you know it," Sloane said, dismissing her defense with a wave of his hand. "I expect my agents to direct all of their resources to the tasks assigned to them, not to waste valuable time and energy on side projects of lesser importance. You need to rethink your priorities."

"Priorities?" Sydney exclaimed, offended by Sloane's callous attitude. She snatched up a paper from the desk and shoved a black-and-white photo of Vicky King in his face. "This woman is dead because some sadistic lunatic is playing a twisted game with me. You can't expect me to sit by and do nothing while this is going on."

"No," he said severely. "I expect you to do your job and locate Oskar Murnau . . . before he launches a devastating attack on the United States." He took the newspaper back from Sydney and laid it face down upon the desk, symbolically burying the murder victim. "Dare I ask what progress you have made regarding Murnau while you've been staking out nightclubs?"

Sydney sat up straight; she was ready for this one. "As it happens, I received a feeler this morning from an online dealer in black market radioactive materials. I've already set up a meeting in Wilmington, Delaware, supposedly to purchase one hundred thousand dollars' worth of illegal neptunium." She handed Sloane a folder containing the details of the proposed operation. "Before tomorrow morning I intend to find out who else he has been dealing with, and where they might be found."

"I see." The news appeared to mollify Sloane somewhat. He sat down behind his desk and reviewed Sydney's proposal. "Yes, this looks promising. Proceed with the meeting, and please keep me informed of any new developments." Assuming the meeting was over, Sydney turned to leave, but Sloane was not done yet. "Sydney, I'm serious about what I said before. I want you to promise me that you'll leave the murder investigation to Nadia and Weiss."

"Of course," she lied.

He nodded, accepting her word, at least on the surface. Did he believe her? Sydney had no way of knowing; the only person who ever really knew what Arvin Sloane was thinking was Sloane himself. Sydney was just happy the meeting was over.

She was almost out of the office, with her hand on the door handle, when Sloane spoke once more. "For what it's worth, Sydney, I regret that young woman's death last night."

So do I, she thought bitterly. Every moment of Vicky King's murder was burned into her memory; she didn't even have to close her eyes to see the killer drive the knife into Vicky's torso once more. A sense of profound regret hung over Sydney, along with massive doses of guilt. According to the newspaper, and Nadia's files, the real Vicky King had worked for a nonprofit environmental group lobbying for tighter controls on toxic waste. She was survived by a mother, a stepfather, two older brothers, and a Siamese cat named Quincy. Sydney tried to imagine the pain Vicky King's loved ones were going through this morning. *All because I once pretended to be a spoiled heiress by the same name.*

Closing the door behind her, Sydney stepped out into the hall, where she found Dixon waiting for her. He cocked his head toward Sloane, who was still visible through the frosted glass partition. "How did it go in there?"

She shrugged her shoulders. Sloane's admonitions meant less than nothing to her. "He approved our plan for the sting operation tonight."

"Good," Dixon said. He accompanied her back toward her cubicle. "We have a lot of prep work to do before we catch a plane to Wilmington. We need to run through every possible contingency and scenario, just in case something goes wrong. I have some concerns about the location. . . ."

Sydney heard Dixon speaking, but her mind was still in that crowded nightclub, chasing after the killer. She tried to remember the face beneath the black biker hat, erratically lit by the colored strobe lights. Who was that woman? The killer knew Sydney, but Syd couldn't return the favor. The woman's dusky complexion reminded Sydney of Maya Rao, an Indian-born assassin Sydney had clashed with several times—most recently in New Orleans—but she'd know Maya if she saw her. And that definitely hadn't been Maya's voice on the bartender's cell phone. *Who else hates me enough to kill innocent women to mess with my head?*

"Sydney?"

Dixon's voice intruded on her thoughts. She realized, with a touch of embarrassment, that she had been tuning him out. "Yes?"

He regarded her skeptically. "I asked you whether your contact expects you to arrive alone."

"Right," she answered, as if she had heard his question the first time. "The deal we worked out is that I'm allowed to bring one armed bodyguard to the meeting. That would be you, of course."

The two agents arrived at her cubicle. A fractal screen saver occupied the face of her monitor. Photos of the five dead women were pinned to her bulletin board, both as a memorial and a reminder. Sydney nudged her mouse, and the floor plans of the meeting site appeared on the monitor. She dropped into her seat, ready to get back to work. "Pull up a chair," she urged Dixon. "The supplier has no idea what *failsafe* looks like, so we have a lot of options where our cover stories are con—"

"Sydney," he interrupted her. "We need to talk."

She could tell by his tone that something was troubling him. "What's on your mind?"

"I'm worried that Sloane may be right," he said gently, lowering his voice so he could not be overheard. "That these murders are distracting you from our primary mission, that they're affecting your ability to concentrate on our assignment." His rich bass voice held only concern, without a trace of condemnation. His sympathetic brown eyes refused to judge her. "We're hunting a very dangerous man, and it's possible that thousands of lives are at stake. As your partner, I need to know that your head is in the game."

Sydney felt a stab of guilt. Defying Sloane was one thing; letting Dixon down was something else altogether. If Dixon thought there was a problem, then she needed to take that seriously. He was her partner, after all.

"I'm sorry," she said softly. "I'd be lying if I said these killings weren't preying on my mind, but you're right. I can't let them interfere with our mission." She looked him in the eye, hoping he could see how sincere she was. "You can count on me. I haven't forgotten about Murnau."

Dixon smiled. "That's all I needed to hear." He drew a chair in closer to Sydney's computer screen. "Now then, let's figure out who we're going to be tonight."

WILMINGTON, DELAWARE

The parking garage was located downtown, not far from the train station. It was nearly three in the morning, so the city streets were practically empty as the black limousine cruised toward the looming concrete garage. A light rain fell softly, causing the avenues and sidewalks to glisten beneath the street-lights. A quarter moon shone through the clouds.

"Phoenix here," Sydney reported from the backseat of the limo. A laptop rested upon her knees. Dixon sat in the driver's seat in front of her, wearing a chauffeur's cap and livery. She peered past his head through the windshield beyond. "We're approaching the rendezvous site."

"Copy that," Vaughn answered her over the comms. He and her father were providing support for this operation, while Sloane and Marshall monitored the situation from Los Angeles, three time zones away. The late-night streets provided few opportunities for concealment, so Vaughn and her dad were hidden inside a parked utility van a block away from the parking garage; in theory, they could be at the garage in seconds if her sting operation went south. Sydney hoped that wouldn't be necessary. "We're tracking you now."

"Thanks," she said. It was good to hear Vaughn's voice, even if it was only a disembodied whisper in her ear. With them each working two cases, on and off the clock, it felt like they had barely seen each other lately, let alone spent quality time together. When they weren't hunting Murnau, they were searching for the alias killer.

Or maybe it was the other way around.

Sydney glanced out the window at the incandescent moon waxing in the dark indigo sky above her. *Only three more nights until the full moon,* she realized. Would Der Werwolf be ready to strike by then? Had he already manufactured all the Black Thorine he needed for his deadly operation? Sydney knew they had to assume the worst: that Murnau was planning a major terrorist attack on July 12. *We have to find him before it's too late.*

"Here we are," Dixon announced, pulling up to

the entrance of the parking garage. A lowered gate blocked the way in. "Are you ready?"

Sydney remembered their talk back in her cubicle. "One hundred percent," she assured him. The night's operation might be their last chance to get a lead on Murnau's current whereabouts before time ran out. She looked at her wristwatch. It was 3:00 A.M. They were right on schedule. "Let's do this."

A sign posted at the entrance read CLOSED FOR REPAIRS. Nevertheless, a surly-looking guard manned the cashier's booth, even at this ungodly hour. A bulge beneath his breast pocket hinted that he was armed. "Can I help you?" he asked gruffly as Dixon rolled down his window to speak with the man. Sydney sat silently in the back.

"They're expecting us," Dixon stated. Latex appliances altered his profile, hiding his angular features beneath prosthetic jowls and a double chin. He handed the guard an index card with a bar code printed on it. The symbol had been e-mailed as a PDF file to Sydney's *failsafe* account by a black-market supplier known only as *meltdown_man*. He or she claimed to have five kilograms of untraceable neptunium-237 to sell. Sydney was anxious to find out who else *meltdown_man* had been dealing with recently.

Like Murnau, perhaps.

The guard ran the index card through a scanner, and a moment later the gate lifted to let them through. "Go to the bottom level," the guard instructed. "He's waiting for you there."

So far, so good.

Dixon drove the limo through the deserted parking garage. Painted yellow arrows led them downward to the lowest level, two stories below the street. The cavernous space was empty except for a single van parked next to a concrete pillar. A Salvation Army logo was painted on the side of the van, but Sydney doubted that the vehicle contained any donated furniture or clothing. A card table and chairs, set up beside the van, provided an incongruous touch. An open bottle of champagne was lodged in an ice bucket atop a white linen tablecloth, flanked by a pair of fluted glasses. The cozy setup looked like it belonged in front of a bistro, not in the middle of a subterranean parking lot in the wee hours of the morning.

How charming, Sydney thought wryly. Nothing went with illegal sales of radioactive materials like a nice glass of bubbly.

She scoped out their surroundings. Concrete

pillars supported the ceiling. Harsh fluorescent lights lit up every corner of the garage, banishing shadows from the site. The vacant lot managed to feel both spacious and claustrophobic at the same time. She could see why *meltdown_man* had chosen this location for the meeting. Without any cars to block the view, there was nothing but open space all around them, which made it hard for either party to stage an ambush. There was no place to spy from, no place to hide, while the underground location further shielded the meeting from inquisitive eyes and ears.

"Looks like this meeting is on," she reported over the comms, but got only static in reply. "Shotgun? Merlin? Do you read me?" She waited in vain for an answer from either Vaughn or Marshall. Chances were, they couldn't hear her, either. Were the dense concrete walls blocking the transmissions, or something else? "Comms are down," she informed Dixon. "We're on our own."

"We've been in this situation before," he reminded her. "Remember that time in Belarus? When we lost contact with our extraction team and had to stow away aboard that refrigerated cargo container?"

Sydney groaned. "Don't remind me. I still shudder whenever I smell caviar." She appreciated his confidence, though. He was right: This was nothing they hadn't faced before. She felt more sorry for Vaughn and her dad, who had to wait in suspense while they were cut off from her. She trusted them to give her time to complete the mission before rushing to her rescue. "All right," she told Dixon. "Let's meet *meltdown_man*."

Dixon honked the horn twice, as prearranged via e-mail. The Salvation Army van honked back to complete the exchange. Two men emerged from the front of the van, both wearing black ski masks. One was skinny and expensively dressed in a gray Armani suit that clashed jarringly with the wool mask. His burly companion, whose size and body language practically screamed bodyguard, wore a lightweight sports jacket, with a Smith & Wesson pistol stuck conspicuously into the waistband of his pants. The smaller man took the lead, carrying a steel canister about the size of a thirty-three-ounce tin of coffee. *The neptunium, perhaps?* Sydney wondered.

"That's our cue," she announced. "It's showtime."

Dixon got out of the limo and walked around to open the door for her. Sydney took her time exiting the car . . . as befitted her current disguise. A silvery wig and old-age makeup gave her the appearance of a sixty-year-old. Her conservative black attire seemed better suited to a funeral than an illicit arms sale. A fur stole was draped around her shoulders. A gauzy black veil hung beneath the brim of her hat, further masking Sydney's true features. She looked like she belonged in *Driving Miss Daisy*, not *Mission: Impossible*.

As far as she knew, she had never met *meltdown_man* before, but after being spotted by Murnau at Edgewood Gardens, she wasn't taking any chances. It was always possible that the German terrorist had provided his associates with a photo or description of her, hence the elaborate disguise. Since Dixon dated back to SD-6 as well, he had also opted for heavier makeup than usual. No one would recognize them tonight.

Or so she hoped.

She walked slowly across the pavement, mimicking the infirmities of age. Another bonus to this alias was that she was likely to catch her opponents by surprise should things come to blows; in a pinch, they'd discover she was pretty spry for an old lady. The laptop was tucked under her arm, while Dixon carried a leather briefcase as he walked behind her. They met their counterparts at the card table, about midway between the two vehicles. Compared to the air-conditioned interior of the limo, the air was warm and humid. Noise from the city above failed to penetrate the sepulchral stillness of the underground garage. Her footsteps echoed hollowly against the dense concrete walls. Dixon set the briefcase down at her feet.

Sydney addressed the skinny man in the Armani suit. "*Meltdown_man*, I presume?" Her voice held the tremulous Yankee twang of an older Katharine Hepburn.

"Just call me Double-M," he replied, laying the steel canister down on top of the table. "*Failsafe*?" Pale blue eyes peered out through the holes in his mask. He had a high voice, white teeth, and an American accent. "I must say, you're not what I expected."

"I should hope not," she said haughtily. "The last thing I would want, when conducting business of this nature, is to fit some crude visual profile."

She sniffed disdainfully as she surveyed their surroundings. "A parking garage at night? Isn't that rather cliché?"

"I prefer to think of it as a reliable standard," he answered breezily. Sydney got the impression that he fancied himself quite the smooth operator. "Certain practices become cliché simply because they prove to have staying power. In any event, I like to think that we've improved on the basic concept." He gestured at the waiting table and champagne. "There's no reason we can't manage our transaction in a civilized manner."

"What about security?" she asked him. The silent comms still troubled her. "Are you quite certain that we are not being monitored?"

"Absolutely." He grinned through his ski mask and lifted the edge of the tablecloth. A blinking electronic gadget, about two feet tall, hummed beneath the table. "A Cerberus V209 jamming device, totally state of the art. As long as this baby is running, our privacy is guaranteed. Hidden bugs, laser microphones . . . you name it, the V209 will shut it down."

Sydney remembered the pen-size jamming device her dad used to employ back at SD-6; it had allowed them to converse privately without fear of electronic eavesdropping, but only for a few minutes at a time. The Cerberus unit was a more powerful version of the same technology. No wonder the comms didn't work.

"We've also taken a few other precautions, just to play it safe." He pointed to a security camera mounted in a nearby corner of the garage. Duct tape was plastered over the unblinking eye of the camera. "Trust me, no one is watching or listening to us."

That's what I was afraid of, she thought. Knowing Marshall, he was probably trying madly to tap into the garage's security system at this very moment. "The setting is satisfactory," she conceded. "Let's proceed with the preliminaries." She gestured toward Dixon. "Allow me to introduce my associate, Sebastian."

By agreement, she and *meltdown_man* were each entitled to one armed bodyguard, but were not allowed to carry weapons themselves. Sydney thought that the faceless supplier had cheated somewhat by installing a second guard upstairs at the cashier's booth, but she chose to overlook that technicality. She wanted to put Double-M at ease before they lowered the boom. *He's not going to see this coming.*

"Bruno," he prompted his bodyguard. The oversize thug loaned his automatic pistol to his boss while he clumsily frisked Sydney for hidden knives or guns. She knew from experience that, thanks to Marshall's high-tech wizardry, her comms were small and discreet enough to evade all but the most rigorous inspection; even so, she suppressed a sigh of relief when Bruno finally stepped away from her and reclaimed his gun.

"She's clean," he grunted. A smirk entered his voice. "Pretty good shape for an old broad."

The impertinent remark failed to ruffle Sydney's feathers. "Well, you know what they say," she said coolly. "Sixty is the new thirty."

She temporarily took custody of Dixon's Beretta while he frisked *meltdown_man* in turn. "Don't touch the mask," the dealer warned. Bruno glowered ominously for emphasis.

"Isn't it a bit late in the year for Halloween?" Sydney teased Double-M. She wondered what he looked like behind the ski mask. *Anybody I'd recognize from the most wanted list?*

He shrugged. "What can I say? I've been spoiled by the intoxicating anonymity of the Internet. These days I don't let anybody see my face."

152

"Must do wonders for your social life," she said drily.

Dixon pronounced Double-M clean as well. Still holding on to his gun, Sydney nodded at the briefcase at her feet. Dixon placed the briefcase on the table, across from the steel canister, and unlocked the clasp. He lifted the lid to reveal neatly stacked piles of American currency. *Meltdown_man*'s eyes lighted up behind his ski mask.

"As agreed, half on delivery, to be paid in unmarked bills," Sydney said, reviewing the terms of the exchange. She slid the briefcase across the table to Double-M, who eagerly started counting the money. Dixon picked up the canister and she laid down her laptop in its place. "The remainder will be transferred electronically to your account once Sebastian has verified that the merchandise is indeed what I paid for."

The skinny supplier examined Dixon. "A chauffeur *and* a chemist? How economical."

"Sebastian has many talents." Sydney took a seat at the table. "It will take him no time at all to test a sample of the merchandise . . . given the proper facilities."

"Have no fear. That's been taken care of."

Double-M sat down opposite her. "Bruno, show Mr. Sebastian to the lab."

The looming bodyguard walked over to the Salvation Army truck and opened the back door of the van, revealing a fully equipped chemical laboratory set up in the rear of the vehicle. Beakers, test tubes, Bunsen burners, a centrifuge, a gas chromatograph, an electron microscope, and other equipment were laid out atop a gleaming, acid-proof counter. An antiradiation suit hung on a hook just inside the back door.

"You see," the supplier bragged. "Everything you need."

Dixon placed the canister on the edge of the van door, then extracted a modified Geiger counter from beneath his double-breasted gaberdine chauffeur's coat. The handheld device resembled a TV remote. "I prefer to use some of my own equipment," he stated, "to ensure that the sensors are calibrated correctly."

"Whatever," Double-M agreed. "That's the real thing, I assure you. I wouldn't think of trying to pull a fast one on you."

In fact, Sydney didn't really care if the canister contained Np-237 or Folgers Crystals, except to the degree that the former would confirm *meltdown_man* as a genuine supplier of black-market neptunium. What she was after was the dealer himself—and whatever info on Murnau he might have tucked away in his brain. All they had to do was take him into custody without anyone getting shot.

"Won't the Cerberus unit interfere with the readings?" she asked. Maybe she could talk Double-M into turning off the jammer?

"I don't see how." He stopped counting his money long enough to give her a quizzical look. "Why, is there a problem?"

Sydney decided not to press the issue. It wasn't worth raising Double-M's suspicions.

"Just a thought," she said casually. "What do I know of science, anyway? That is what I pay people like Sebastian for."

While Dixon went through the motions of prepping for lab work under the watchful eye of Bruno, Sydney attempted to draw *meltdown_man* into a conversation. "So tell me, is there a large demand for neptunium these days?"

"Large enough," he said vaguely. "Can I pour you some champagne?"

"Please," Sydney answered graciously. She

opened up her laptop and switched on the power. Presumably, Double-M intended to turn off the jammer when it came time to transfer the funds to his offshore account. "Do you have many other customers?"

He poured himself a glass of bubbly as well. "Are you testing me? You should know better than to ask me about my other clients. I am famously discreet."

We'll see about that, she thought. She took a sip of the champagne, then grimaced and clutched her chest. She whimpered in pain.

Alarm showed through the dealer's mask. "What's the matter?"

"My heart," she gasped. The champagne glass slipped from her fingers and crashed to the ground, spilling champagne on the pavement. Trembling, she fished a plastic pill container from her pocket. Her palsied fingers struggled with the safety cap. "Wretched childproof lids! . . ."

Over by the van, Bruno turned toward the commotion at the table. "Excuse me," Dixon said, distracting him. He thrust the hood of the radiation suit at the bodyguard. "Would you mind holding this for a minute?" Caught off guard, Bruno accepted the hood with his free hand. His puzzled eyes shifted between the table and Dixon, uncertain which way they should be looking.

With a convulsive motion, Sydney wrenched open the container, only to lose her grip on the vial. Dozens of purple capsules spilled out onto the pavement. "My pills!" She leaned over to reach for them, but was halted by what appeared to be another agonizing spasm. Moaning pitifully, she collapsed against the back of her seat. Her artificially aged face twisted in agony. "Help me . . . my medication! . . ."

"Allow me!" Double-M insisted. Terrified, perhaps, of his customer expiring before she could complete the transaction, he jumped from his seat and knelt down onto the floor beside the table. "Hang on!" he pleaded frantically as he started scooping up the scattered pills. "I've got them!"

"Excuse me," Dixon asked Bruno. He tugged at the radiation hood to get the bodyguard's attention. His personal Geiger counter rested a few feet away, on the floor of the van. "Can I have the hood back?"

Double-M hurriedly collected the loose pills into his palm as Sydney took hold of her laptop with both hands and brought it down hard against the back of his head. Sturdy carbon fiber collided with the flesh and bone beneath the man's wool mask. He dropped face-first onto the asphalt.

"What the—!" Bruno exclaimed. He raised his gun, but not soon enough. Sydney turned the back of the keyboard toward the startled bodyguard and pressed the escape key. A gas-propelled dart shot from the rear of the computer, striking Bruno in the chest. He winced in pain and glanced down at the dart in surprise. He yanked the missile from his chest, but a potent tranquilizer was already coursing through his bloodstream. The dart slipped from his fingers, along with the gun in his other hand, and he grabbed on to Dixon for support as his entire body went limp. He toppled over onto Dixon, who staggered beneath the bodybuilder's weight. Bruno's eyes rolled up until only the whites were visible, and his jaw sagged open.

So much for the bodyguard, Sydney thought. *Now we can really get down to business.*

She peered down at *meltdown_man*, who also looked dead to the world. Maybe she shouldn't have hit him so hard? She didn't want to wait until later to get the answers she needed. "All right," she said, dropping the patrician accent. "No more playacting." She put down the computer and took hold of the champagne bottle. Rather than let the remaining bubbly go to waste, she poured the contents of the bottle onto the unconscious trader's head. "Rise and shine!"

The liquid doused Double-M, reviving him. "Huh?" he sputtered as he lifted his soaked head from the pavement. Purple capsules, containing nothing but a placebo, were strewn around his prone form. He lifted himself onto all fours, and probed the back of his head with one hand. His battered brain slowly put the pieces together. "Sonofabitch! You hit me!"

"I'll do more than that if you don't tell me what I need to know." Syd stood over him, clutching the empty bottle by its neck. Channeling her father, she imbued her voice with understated menace. "I strongly recommend that you cooperate."

But the masked trader was more resourceful than she had expected. Recovering from the blow with surprising speed, he kicked backward with one leg, knocking Sydney's legs out from under her. She fell backward into her empty chair, which crashed to the ground beneath her. The overturned metal seat didn't exactly make for a soft landing; she yelped in pain as her back collided with the underside of the chair. The champagne bottle shattered against the asphalt.

She was going to have some ugly bruises in the morning, but she didn't care about that just then. Lifting her head, she saw Double-M spring to his feet and dash for the van, leaving the money behind. Sydney scrambled up from the pavement and took off after him, only to trip on the overturned chair. She stumbled forward, skinning her knee on the blacktop, as the fugitive arms dealer climbed into the driver's seat of the van.

"Outrigger!" she called out, but her partner was still handcuffing the tranquilized bodyguard. He shoved Bruno's body away from him and reclaimed his Geiger counter.

The van's engine roared to life and Sydney found herself caught in the glare of the truck's headlights. The truck lunged forward, veering straight toward her, and she dove out of the way, looking like the world's nimblest senior citizen.

Bruno was not so lucky. Desperate to escape, his employer reversed right over the unconscious bodyguard. The fleeing van didn't even slow down as it sped toward the exit ramp leading out of the underground parking garage. Rolling to her feet, Sydney assessed the vehicle that was rapidly getting away from them.

She didn't run for her own car. Weiss had already fulfilled the week's quota for high-speed chases. Instead, she shouted to Dixon.

"Zap him!"

"Already on it!" he called back. Raising his supposed Geiger counter, he aimed the hand-held device at the fleeing van. A powerful microwave beam targeted the vehicle, frying the microchips wired into its fuel injection system and other controls. The energy spike caused the van's engine to stall immediately. Sydney watched with satisfaction as the van coasted to a stop. Marshall's latest gadget had performed just as he'd promised.

This definitely beats shooting out the tires, she thought.

Sparing only a moment to wince at Bruno's crushed body, Sydney took possession of the body-guard's Smith & Wesson and then she and Dixon converged on the van from both sides. Dixon had his own Beretta raised and ready. Sydney hoped that Double-M didn't have an extra weapon stowed inside the van.

"FBI!" she lied, knowing that the Bureau would deny it later. She warily approached the door by the driver's seat. "Step out with your hands up!" Double-M refused to budge, so she fired a warning shot through the side-view mirror. Broken glass went flying.

That did the trick. "Okay! All right!" the arms dealer yelled from inside the van. The door swung open and he stumbled out onto the pavement, holding his hands above his head. Frightened eyes bulged out from behind his mask. "Don't shoot!"

Dixon rushed around to cover Sydney as she strode forward and shoved their prisoner against the side of the van. She quickly patted him down for hidden weapons, but found nothing more lethal than a cell phone, which she confiscated. They could search its memory later, after she was through with the man himself.

"Talk fast!" she warned Double-M, ripping off his soggy ski mask. His face was bland and nondescript, the kind you forget five minutes after seeing it. He was flushed and sweaty, his dirty blond hair plastered to his skull. Tears leaked from his eyes.

Snot ran from his nose and he reeked of spilled champagne. "Who else has been in the market for neptunium-237?"

"Nobody!" he insisted unconvincingly. His shifty eyes avoided hers. His voice grew shriller by the moment. "I have the right to remain silent! I want my lawyer!"

Sydney showed him no mercy. "You're dealing in outlawed nuclear materials during a time of war. We could shoot you on the spot and nobody would make a peep." She plucked off her veil so he could see just how serious she was. "Now answer my questions before I decide to force-feed you the neptunium in that canister. Who else have you sold Np-237 to?"

She heard footsteps from above as the guard from the ticket booth came running down the entrance ramp. *He must have heard the gunshot,* Sydney realized. Dixon eliminated the threat with a single shot from his Beretta.

Double-M swallowed hard. "Okay, there was one guy," he admitted. "But I never knew his name, I swear!"

She extracted a photo of Murnau from her pocket. "Is this him?"

"Yes, yes!" He nodded energetically. By now his suave manner had completely evaporated. "That's the guy. He ordered ten kilograms a few weeks back."

Right after he got the formula for Black Thorine, Sydney guessed. "Do you know where he is now?"

"Maybe," he hedged. "He paid extra to have me smuggle it out of the country for him. The final destination was some winery outside Barcelona." Sweat streamed down his face as he pleaded pathetically. "Look, maybe we can make some sort of deal? I'm doing my best to cooperate with you guys here. Give me a break, okay?"

Right, she thought. *Like that's going to happen.* After watching him run over his own bodyguard, she wasn't inclined to cut Double-M any slack. Bruno's pulped body wasn't even cold yet. *I have a better idea.*

Without warning, she pistol-whipped her prisoner, knocking him out cold. He crumpled onto the pavement.

She turned toward Dixon, who lowered his gun and walked over to the card table. Pills and broken glass littered the asphalt. Lifting the tablecloth, he switched off the jamming device. "Outrigger to Shotgun," he announced. "We have the package. You can come pick us up."

"Copy that," Vaughn replied, sounding relieved. "Good to hear from you."

Sydney used Double-M's belt to tie his hands behind his back. *Barcelona,* she thought. Part of her hated the idea of leaving the country while the alias killer was still at large in Los Angeles, but what could she do? Duty called.

"Tell headquarters to send a jet. We're going to Barcelona."

CHAPTER 8

SAN FERNANDO VALLEY

The run-down apartment building looked like it had seen better days. Graffiti defaced the sooty stucco walls of the complex, the meager lawn was clotted with weeds and badly in need of mowing, and garbage littered the sidewalk. The light from a solitary streetlamp fell upon a sign reading ACIENDA ARMS. Vaughn guessed that an *H* had gone missing.

"Looks like Ms. Fretz has fallen on hard times," Jack commented as he pulled up to the curb in front of the building. Control freak that he was, Sydney's dad had insisted on driving. Michael

167

Vaughn sat in the passenger seat beside him. They had left APO shortly after 7:30 P.M., missing the rush hour traffic.

"So it seems," Vaughn agreed. "Let's hope she's at home."

Despite their best efforts, he and Jack had been unable to track down Lewis Fretz himself. That wasn't particularly surprising, considering that Fretz was an expert in manufacturing false identities; if he wanted to go deep underground, he certainly knew how to do so. However, they had managed to locate the address of his ex-wife, one Marlene Fretz. With any luck, she could give them a lead on her former spouse, Sydney's onetime coworker at SD-6.

Vaughn hoped they weren't wasting their time. "You still think Fretz is a suspect?" he asked aloud. "Sydney and Nadia saw a woman murder Victoria King. Weiss saw the same woman escape on a motorcycle."

"True," Jack admitted, "but that doesn't mean Lewis Fretz isn't still involved with the murders somehow. The woman at the nightclub could have been a girlfriend, an accomplice, a hired killer, or maybe even Fretz himself in disguise." He turned off the car's engine. "He'd hardly be the only cross-dresser hitting the clubs in West Hollywood."

Jack's got a point there, Vaughn thought. He recalled the slim, androgynous individual pictured in Fretz's photographs; it was possible that the elusive suspect could have passed for female, especially in the chaotic environment of the club. Sydney had mentioned blaring music and colored strobe lights. "Well, let's see what his ex has to say."

Exiting the car, they approached the entrance to the 'Acienda Arms. A handwritten note taped by the door informed them that the building's intercom was out of order. Vaughn jiggled the handle on the front door, which clicked open without much effort on his part. "Impressive security," he remarked sarcastically.

Jack glanced around at the low-rent appearance of the complex. "You get what you pay for."

The foyer looked just as shabby as the building's exterior. The dingy carpet hadn't been vacuumed in days. Cigarette burns had left scorch marks on the fabric. Plaster was peeling off the walls, exposing glimpses of naked insulation. A large brown water stain had spread across the ceiling. The stagnant air smelled of tobacco and mildew.

"Lovely," Jack commented. No doubt Marlene Fretz had enjoyed better accommodations back when her husband had been gainfully employed by SD-6. Her situation had undoubtedly gone downhill since then. Defunct terrorist cells seldom offered generous severance packages.

According to the rows of miniature mailboxes mounted to the wall, M. Fretz resided in Apartment 2C. The box in question was empty; apparently, Marlene had already picked up today's mail. *Too bad*, Vaughn thought. They might have learned something by leafing through her correspondence. Maybe she still received mail from her ex-husband?

That might be worth checking out in the future, he thought. *Plus, sifting through a stranger's mail won't be very difficult to hide from Sloane—it's a pretty low-tech spy tactic.*

Jack and Vaughn took the stairs to the second floor. A loose banister wobbled alarmingly. "Watch your step," he warned Jack.

"Thank you, Agent Vaughn, but I'm perfectly capable of navigating a flight of stairs on my own." Jack's tone was even frostier than usual. "You may be interested to know that I once managed to scale the Berlin Wall without your assistance."

Vaughn was tempted to point out that the wall had been history for more than fifteen years, but he held his tongue. No doubt the alias killings had Sydney's dad on edge. Vaughn wasn't in love with the idea of his girlfriend's proxies being murdered on a regular basis either. Not only did each new killing add to Sydney's emotional anguish, but Vaughn had to wonder how long the killer would be content to murder her namesakes before coming after Sydney herself. Was Sydney Bristow the final name on the killer's hit list?

Not if I can help it, he thought. With Sydney now en route to Barcelona with Dixon, and unable to investigate the murders on her own, Vaughn felt more pressure than ever to nab the killer on her behalf. *I'll feel a whole lot better if we stop these killings before Syd gets back from Europe.*

Jack had to be feeling the same way.

They walked down a squalid hallway toward Marlene's apartment. Noises from her neighbors' units invaded the hall through the paper-thin walls. A chorus of crying babies, angry voices, and blaring television sets followed the two agents all the way to 2C. Vaughn was relieved to hear a TV playing inside the apartment; Marlene seemed to be at home. He was glad that they hadn't driven to the Valley for nothing.

Now they just had to hope that the trip was worth it.

Fretz may have nothing to do with the killings, Vaughn reminded himself. They couldn't rule out the possibility that Oskar Murnau was behind the murders instead. Maybe the woman at the club had been a replacement for the late Kimber Gill?

In which case, this whole trip is a wild goose chase.

Jack rapped firmly on the flimsy plywood door. Vaughn kept to the left of the door, out of sight. He wasn't expecting an armed response from Marlene Fretz, but it didn't pay to take chances. When no one responded, Jack knocked again, more forcefully this time.

"Who is it?" a voice called out irritably from inside.

"Ms. Fretz?" Jack raised his voice. "Can you please come to the door? I'd like to talk to you about your former husband."

"Go to hell!"

Vaughn and Jack exchanged a look. This didn't bode well.

"I'm afraid that's not an option," Jack insisted. His tone made it clear he wasn't going anywhere. "This is an official matter."

A pointed obscenity escaped 2C. Footsteps came toward them and the door opened a crack. Suspicious blue eyes peered past the copper chain holding the door shut. Vaughn got a glimpse of mousy brown hair and a sallow complexion. Cigarette smoke tickled his nostrils. "Make it snappy," a raspy voice demanded. "What's this all about?"

"Marlene Fretz?" Jack inquired.

"That's me," she confirmed. "This better not be another damn subpoena. I'll sue you Feds for harassment. Why can't you just leave me alone, for God's sake?"

Vaughn guessed that she had been thoroughly grilled by the FBI, the CIA, or both. Probably more than once. That's what happens when your spouse gets accused of taking part in international espionage.

"I'm sorry to disturb you," Jack said. His face maintained a neutral expression. "My partner and I are with the parole department. We're trying to locate your former husband."

"You think I know where he is?" Bitter amusement rang in her voice. "That's a laugh. I don't know where that poor, sad bastard is. What's more, I don't care anymore."

She tried to close the door, but Jack put his foot in the way. His voice took on a subtly menacing tone. "You would be well advised to cooperate with us, Ms. Fretz. The government takes your ex-husband's activities very seriously, and will not look kindly on any attempts to stonewall us."

Guess Jack's the bad cop tonight, Vaughn realized. To be honest, he wasn't sure that Jack was even capable of playing the good cop in an interrogation. His icy, intimidating persona wasn't exactly suited to putting people at ease.

Marlene got the message. "Okay, okay." She unhooked the chain and stepped out into the hall. She was a medium-size brunette with hazel eyes, freckles, and a sour expression. She was still in decent shape, but tobacco and hard times had taken its toll on her jaundiced complexion. She was wearing a terry cloth bathrobe and slippers, and her arms were crossed defensively against her chest. A lit cigarette was pinched between her nicotine-stained fingers.

Vaughn noted that she hardly matched the description of the tall, dark-skinned woman who had killed Vicky King two nights ago. Then again, Sydney changed her appearance all the time. *I wonder if Marlene knows how to ride a motorcycle?* he wondered. He hadn't seen a Harley parked out front.

A doorway opened down the hall and an elderly man in an undershirt and boxer shorts stepped out to see what was going on. "What are you looking at?" she shouted at the nosy neighbor. "Mind your own goddamn business!"

The old man retreated back into his apartment. It occurred to Vaughn that he and Jack might want to go door-to-door with Lewis Fretz's photo later on. Maybe one of the neighbors had seen him coming or going from Marlene's apartment?

It couldn't hurt to find out.

"Look, I already told you," she said sullenly. "I don't know where Lewis is." She took a drag on her cigarette and blew the smoke in Jack's face. "How come I have to keep getting raked over the coals like this? I didn't do anything. He was the spy, not me! Hell, I thought he was working at that bank the whole time. He lied to me for years."

Vaughn felt a twinge of sympathy. He knew what it was like to find yourself married to a traitor. So did Jack, for that matter. He wondered if Marlene had always been this touchy, or if the events of the past few years were responsible for her sour attitude and her open hostility. *Lauren's betrayal left me pretty bitter,* he recalled. *And I didn't end up living in a dump like this.*

"I understand," he said gently. "You've gotten a raw deal. Of course you're not responsible for your ex-husband's crimes. No one is blaming you for anything. You're the victim here, and I really hate to put you through this one more time. Unfortunately, you're the only lead we've got." His soulful eyes implored her. "Are you absolutely sure you can't help us somehow? We'd really appreciate it."

His sympathetic tone had the desired effect. Marlene's tense posture relaxed a bit. "Look, you've got to understand something. Lewis had no idea what was really going on at SD-6. Sloane and the others played him for a sucker. Then, afterward, he just . . . fell apart. He couldn't cope with being accused of treason, of finding out that he had been used all those years. Lewis always thought he was so clever; discovering that he had been fooled so easily came as a terrible blow to him. He became convinced that the government was trying to railroad him, which just made things worse. They ended up throwing the book at him. By the time he got out of prison, he was a wreck, psychologically."

Her eyes moistened and she dabbed at them with her knuckles. "I tried to stand by him, I swear, but it was no good. He wouldn't listen to me. All he ever talked about was getting back at the people who had screwed him over. He started drinking too much. He couldn't hold down a job. . . ." Her voice caught in her throat. "I wanted to help him through this, even though he had been lying to me for years, but he wouldn't let me. He wasn't the same man anymore. Finally, I just had to get out." She snorted at her decrepit surroundings. "You can see how well that's working for me."

Vaughn remembered kissing Sydney amid the ruins of SD-6, the day they brought the organization down. Apparently, that was the same day Lewis Fretz's life had started to come apart. Vaughn felt guilty for not paying closer attention to the human costs of that operation. *There was no other choice,* he reminded himself. SD-6, and the rest of the Alliance, had needed to be destroyed. Besides, Dixon and Marshall had landed on their feet afterward, along with most of the other unsuspecting employees of SD-6. Whose fault was it that Lewis Fretz hadn't been able to do the same?

"Do you know where he is now?" Jack pressed.

She shook her head. "I haven't heard from him in months."

Vaughn noticed that she averted her eyes before answering. "Are you certain?" He considered her impoverished circumstances. "It's possible that we may be able to come up with some sort of reward."

Jack arched an eyebrow, but said nothing. Vaughn knew Sydney's dad had untraceable funds stashed away all over the world.

"Reward?" Marlene's eyes lit up. She took a puff on her cigarette as she contemplated Vaughn's offer. She seemed to be wrestling with some internal dilemma. "Wait a second," she said unconvincingly. "Come to think of it, there's something I probably ought to show you. Don't go away."

She stepped back into her apartment, shutting

the door behind her. Despite the lack of privacy in the hall, she was apparently in no hurry to invite them into her home. Vaughn wondered if she was embarrassed by her apartment.

A minute later Marlene emerged from 2C once more, sans cigarette. She held out an open shoe box filled with legal-size envelopes. Her current address was typed on the front of the envelopes. "I started getting these about a month ago," she explained, after looking up and down the hall to make sure none of her neighbors were listening. "I just got the top one this morning."

Vaughn picked up the envelope that rested at the top of the stack. Inside he found a news clipping freshly scissored from one of the local tabloids. He recognized the headline immediately: GIRL-ON-GIRL MURDER: FATAL STABBING AT W. HOLLYWOOD NIGHT SPOT.

What followed was a rather sensationalistic account of Vicky King's murder at Mythos. Vaughn handed the clipping over to Jack, then quickly sorted through the rest of the envelopes. Just as he feared, he found multiple articles on the preceding murders, dating all the way back to the grisly death of Kate Jones five weeks before. All together, the envelopes contained a veritable scrapbook-in-the-making of the alias killings.

Looks like we're on the right track, Vaughn thought. *This trip wasn't a waste after all.*

Jack scowled as he inspected the clippings, then glared accusingly at Marlene. "And you didn't feel obliged to report this to the authorities?"

"So they can throw Lewis back into prison?" Marlene said defensively. "Or shoot him down in the streets like a mad dog?" She gripped the box tightly, as if unwilling to let it go. "Just because I divorced the guy, that doesn't mean I want to sic the police on him. Besides, why would Lewis want to hurt these women? It doesn't make any sense!"

Vaughn examined the envelopes. None of them featured a return address or any handwriting samples. "How do you know these letters came from your ex-husband?"

"I don't!" Marlene blurted out, seizing on that argument. "I just assumed . . . I mean, how many nutcases do I know? Lewis was the only—" She cut herself off in midsentence, as though she has said too much already. "But that doesn't prove anything."

Jack eyed her suspiciously. "Do the names of

the victims have any significance to you?"

"Not at all," she insisted. "I've never heard of any of these women before. There's no reason for Lewis to hurt any of them." Without warning, she snatched the clippings out of Jack's hands. "Trust me, I was married to him for twelve years. He's not a serial killer, just a poor jerk who took the fall for something that wasn't even his fault!"

She sounded sincere. She obviously still cared about Fretz to some degree.

"We're going to need those articles," Vaughn informed her. He tightened his grip on the empty envelopes. "For fingerprinting and such."

Marlene clutched the clippings to her chest. "Do you have a warrant?"

APO never bothered with warrants, but Vaughn didn't want to have to wrestle the articles away from Marlene in the hallway, where the neighbors would hear. *What's the best way to handle this?*

Jack took out his wallet. He offered Marlene a couple of hundred-dollar bills. "Perhaps these will suffice?"

Marlene hesitated, then traded the clippings for the money. Her face held a pained expression; Vaughn could tell this was costing her.

"Thank you," Jack said brusquely. He handed the clippings over to Vaughn, who returned them to their original envelopes. Jack drew a few more bills from his wallet. "Is there anything else we ought to see?"

"Well . . ." Marlene looked hungrily at the proffered C-notes. At this point, there seemed little reason for her stonewalling them any further. "There is one more thing." She backed into her apartment, taking the shoe box with her. Once again she conspicuously declined to invite them inside. "Stay right there."

Moments later she returned bearing a narrow, rectangular box of the sort used to hold business cards. A sample card was taped to the lid. "Take a look at this," Marlene said, handing the box to Vaughn. "I'm not sure if this is quite what you're looking for, but it should give you an idea of just how far gone Lewis is."

Vaughn inspected the sample card. The embossed type read:

LEWIS M. FRETZ
Loan Officer
Credit Dauphine

Vaughn recognized the name of the company. Credit Dauphine was a banking firm that had once served as a cover for SD-6. Sydney had supposedly worked for the same company.

Inside the box was a generous supply of identical cards. They looked brand-new.

"Lewis had those printed up a year ago, after he got out of prison. Years after the Feds shut down SD-6," Marlene stated. She shuddered at the memory. "It was like he couldn't bring himself to admit that that part of his life was over, that he couldn't just pick up where he left off. To tell you the truth, it scared the daylights out of me. It was one of the reasons I finally left him."

I can see that, Vaughn thought. Fretz was sounding more and more disturbed. But disturbed enough to be behind the alias killings?

The clippings certainly seemed to point toward that conclusion.

Jack looked unimpressed by the useless business cards, but he paid Marlene anyway. "Thank you, Ms. Fretz. If you think of anything else, or if your ex-husband contacts you, please call us immediately."

He handed Marlene a bogus business card of

his own. Vaughn knew that the number on the card matched a cell phone number for a line Jack had acquired expressly for this investigation. As far as they knew, Sloane was unaware of the phone line's existence.

"One more question," Jack added. "Does the name Sydney Bristow mean anything to you?"

"Who?" Marlene said. She appeared to search her memory. "Wait a sec, wasn't that some girl who used to work at the bank with Lewis? I think I met her at a Christmas party once." A worried look came over her face. "She hasn't been murdered too, has she?"

"No," Jack said tersely. "Not yet."

The agents let Marlene return to her television and walked down the hall. "Well?" Jack asked Vaughn in a low voice. "What was your impression of Ms. Fretz?"

"She clearly didn't want to let us into her apartment," Vaughn answered. He glanced back over his shoulder at the door to 2C. "You don't think she's got Fretz in there, do you?" He asked, half joking.

Jack shook his head. "If I thought that was a possibility, we would be ransacking the apartment right now. Still, despite her eventual show of cooperation, I'm not entirely convinced that she told us everything. She may very well be in touch with Fretz." He frowned, obviously frustrated despite all the progress they had made. "Unfortunately, we lack the resources to place Ms. Fretz under twenty-four-hour surveillance."

Vaughn made a mental note to quietly inform Weiss and Nadia about the mysterious envelopes and their contents. They needed to know that somebody was keeping Marlene Fretz up to date on the alias killings. "So now what?"

Jack rapped on the door to 2A. "Now we talk to the neighbors."

CHAPTER 9

SANT SADURNí
SPAIN

Sydney had read somewhere that there were more acres of vineyards in Spain than in any other country in the world. *I can believe it,* she thought as she and Dixon walked silently through the Penedès wine region south of Barcelona. A gibbous moon shone down on acres of rolling hills and green valleys. Rows of tended vines shielded the agents from sight. A warm breeze rustled the leaves all around them. Sydney plucked a grape from a nearby vine and popped it into her mouth. Not quite ripe, it was tart enough to make her lips pucker.

Too bad I'm not here for the wine, she thought.

They advanced on their target: a sprawling stone building situated on a hill overlooking the vineyards. Under duress, *meltdown_man* (real name: Dennis Muckerheide) had confessed to shipping ten kilograms of neptunium to this specific location. Velaquez Winery was housed in a converted monastery dating back to the twelfth century. A modest stone cathedral abutted the abbey's enclosed cloisters, refectory, chapter house, and dormitory. Stained glass windows overlooked the grounds surrounding the building. Steam rose from vents in the peaked slate roof above the former cathedral. Signs printed in both Spanish and Catalan read NO TRESPASSING.

Like that's going to stop us, Sydney thought.

Sydney glanced up at the sky. Only one more day until the full moon. Had Murnau already managed to manufacture all the Black Thorine he needed? She hoped not; according to Marshall's calculations, Der Werwolf had enough Np-237 to produce at least six liters of the dreaded superexplosive. Given that just a single drop was enough to wipe out an entire city block, that was a terrifying prospect. The damage Murnau could inflict with that much Black Thorine was incomprehensible.

Reaching the edge of the field, which was ten yards away from the winery's main building, they crouched down between the vines. A graveled courtyard separated them from the high stone walls of the onetime monastery. Enormous stainless steel tanks, eight feet in diameter, filled the courtyard, along with forklifts and stacks of wooden pallets. A huge steel press, capable of holding many tons of grapes at one time, rested on the gravel, next to an automated stemmer/crusher. Peering between the tanks, Sydney spied several cars and trucks parked in front of the winery. Lights inside the building illuminated the stained glass windows on the top floor of the old cathedral.

"Looks like a busy night at the winery," she whispered to Dixon. Matte black fatigues helped them blend with the shadows. Lightweight backpacks held vital op-tech. Night vision goggles added an eerie green tint to the scene. A black woolen cap kept Sydney's hair tucked away. "Seems like an awful lot of activity for the middle of the night." Somehow she doubted that there was an exclusive midnight wine tasting going on.

"Phoenix to Merlin," she reported back to headquarters. "Target is in sight."

"Copy that, Phoenix," Marshall replied. "Or should I say *buenas noches*?"

It occurred to Sydney that it was still daylight where Marshall was; Barcelona was nine hours ahead of Los Angeles. She couldn't help worrying about what was going on back home while she was in Spain. Was the alias killer preparing to strike again?

She knew that Nadia and Weiss were on the case at that very moment. Just the same, her heart sank at the thought of yet another blameless young woman falling victim to the murderer's twisted agenda. Without any prompting, her memory replayed that awful moment back at Mythos; in her mind's eye she once again saw the quartz knife sink into Vicky King's unsuspecting flesh. *I couldn't even stop the killer when she was only a few feet away,* she worried. *What good am I now that I'm fifteen hours away from L.A.?*

"Sydney?" Dixon's voice brought her back to the matter at hand. His concerned eyes searched her face. "Are you with me?"

She blushed, embarrassed to realize that she

had let the killings get to her again. *Knock it off,* she scolded herself. There was nothing she could do about the murders right now. *Keep your mind on the mission.* Tonight was all about catching Murnau.

"You have the coordinates, Merlin," she stated crisply, once again all business. "Can you give us a head count?"

"Your wish is my command," Marshall replied. Overhead, an orbiting spy satellite beamed infrared photos of the winery straight to APO. "Not counting you two, I'm reading twenty-three warm bodies on the scene. Four posted outside the building, nineteen more inside."

"Copy that, Merlin," Sydney acknowledged. Too bad they couldn't tell for sure whether one of those warm bodies belonged to Oskar Murnau. They would have to find that out for themselves, despite the guards outside.

The size of the crowd inside the winery concerned her. They had not anticipated so many possible adversaries at this time of night. Contacting the local authorities for reinforcements was not an option; the CIA was in no hurry to let Black Thorine fall into the hands of foreign intelligence.

"What about the cellars?" Dixon asked. Advance intel had revealed that the monastery's ancient catacombs had long ago been converted into wine cellars.

"Nada," Marshall reported. "Everybody's working the ground floor, or else standing guard inside. Nothing down in the cellars but mice and spiders, probably." His voice took on an enthusiastic tone. "Hey, have you tried checking out my handy-dandy Black Thorine detector yet?"

"We were just getting to that," Dixon said. He retrieved the device from Sydney's backpack. The handheld scanner resembled the phony Geiger counter he had used back at the parking garage in Delaware; instead of emitting microwaves, however, this device was intended to detect the presence of Black Thorine from approximately two hundred yards away. Sydney was impressed that Marshall had managed to come up with a portable version so quickly. But would the experimental prototype function in the field?

Time to find out, Sydney thought.

Dixon activated the scanner. Designed for stealth operations, the device emitted no telltale clicks or beeps, but a faint green glow radiated from the lighted display panel. Dixon pointed the device at the winery, shifting position slightly in order to aim the scanner between two fifteen-hundred-gallon steel tanks. He stared intently at the readout on the glowing panel.

"So?" Sydney asked expectantly.

Dixon looked up from the display, a sober expression upon his face. "Pay dirt. They're definitely making more than wine in there."

"I can never remember," she quipped, "does Black Thorine go with red meat or fish?" Her flippant remark masked her dismay at confirming that Murnau had indeed succeeded in synthesizing the outlawed explosive. "Can you tell where exactly they're storing the chemical?"

He fiddled with the controls, trying to zero in on the precise location of the Black Thorine. "It's no good," he said after a few minutes. "I can't get an exact fix on the location, not at this range." He continued to struggle with the recalcitrant device. "Merlin?"

"Sorry, guys," Marshall replied, sounding mortified. "I'm not sure what the problem is. Maybe you're getting some background radiation from their stockpile of isotopic thorium? I'm going to have to take a closer look at the prototype when you get back." Sydney could readily imagine his chagrined expression. "This really bites. I hate to let you guys down."

"It's all right," Sydney insisted. "You've already figured out a way to detect a supposedly undetectable substance . . . and in just a couple of weeks. That's a miracle."

"You really think so?" he said, brightening. "Because, you know, I can probably fine-tune the tracking mechanism once I get the chance. The basic theory is sound. All it needs is a little more work."

"I know you can," she assured him. "In the meantime, we've figured out the most important thing. There's Black Thorine on the premises."

Just what we didn't want to discover, she thought glumly. If only they could have caught up with Murnau before he'd had a chance to manufacture the explosive! This mission had just become much more complicated. *We've got two objectives now: capture Murnau and seize his entire supply of Black Thorine. Not necessarily in that order.*

"We should split up," Sydney suggested, turning to Dixon. "You take the detector and check out the catacombs. Maybe he's got the Black Thorine stored down there." She rose from her crouch. It felt good to stretch her legs. "I'll find out what's going on upstairs and see if Murnau himself is in attendance."

Dixon raised no objections to her plan. "Be careful," he advised her. "Remember, we're seriously outnumbered here. Don't try to forcibly extract Murnau on your own."

Sydney felt a twinge of guilt as she recalled that her father and Vaughn had elected to stay behind in Los Angeles. Sloane had originally planned to send both men to Barcelona as well, to provide backup for this operation, but her dad had argued against that deployment on the grounds that, since Murnau's ultimate target would almost surely be on American soil, it would be a mistake to have all of APO's senior agents tied up in Europe. What if APO suddenly got word of an imminent attack on some location in the U.S.?

That had been his official argument, anyway; Sydney suspected that he'd wanted to stay in Los Angeles so he and Vaughn could keep tracking the alias killer, for her sake. *I'm the reason we're on our own here.*

"We may have to just keep an eye on Murnau tonight," Dixon continued, "and grab him later when he's not so heavily guarded."

"Uh-huh." Sydney made no promises. She wasn't going to take any reckless chances, but if the opportunity arose to separate Murnau from his men, she intended to make the most of it. She hadn't forgotten how he had callously gunned down that innocent tourist back at the hedge garden in Pennsylvania. Der Werwolf needed to be caged— permanently. "Watch out for yourself," she whispered to Dixon. "And good luck."

Dixon vanished into the shadowy vineyards, leaving Sydney alone at the fringe of the courtyard. She gave him a few minutes to get clear, just in case she accidentally exposed herself, then sprinted out from between the vine-covered trellises. Listening intently for the footsteps of the guards, she used the looming steel tanks for cover, darting from behind one tank to another until she reached the high limestone wall of the bell tower at the rear of the cathedral. She heard a sentry pacing restlessly just around the corner. A whiff of tobacco divulged that the guard was enjoying a smoke while he kept watch. Sydney hoped not to disturb him.

She waited until the footsteps were moving away from her, then glanced up at the weathered stone wall rising before her. Roughly forty-five feet overhead, a stained glass window, depicting some long-dead saint, glowed with a heavenly radiance. *That's my way in,* she decided.

A jutting stone cornice, several feet above the window, provided a ready target for the grapnel gun in Sydney's backpack. Seizing the device, she fired a CO_2-propelled dart, attached to a monofilament decel cable, into the cornice. The microdiamond drill head dug deeply into the ancient masonry, securing the line. She tugged once on the line to make sure it was secure, then affixed the line to her belt and flicked a switch on the launcher. A motorized winch lifted her off her feet as the retracting line carried her upward.

Within seconds she was hanging outside the stained glass window. Peering through the colored glass, she spotted an elevated catwalk on the other side of the window. *Perfect.* Applying acid around the border of the portrait, she began to carefully remove the stained-glass from its frame. The acid hissed and bubbled as it went to work.

The sound of footsteps below caught her

attention. Looking down, she saw a guard come around the corner. To her dismay, he paused directly beneath her, forty-plus feet below. *Don't look up,* she silently urged the man as he puffed on a particularly pungent cigar. The smoke from his stogie rose upward, irritating her nostrils, and she had to pinch her nose to keep from sneezing.

Acutely aware of her close proximity to the oblivious guard, Sydney gently eased the stained glass window onto the catwalk inside the tower. She tensed as she let go of the pane, not wanting the tinkling of broken glass to reach the guard's ears, but the stained glass portrait stayed in one piece. Relieved, she climbed onto the window ledge and unclipped the cable from her belt.

So long, pal, she thought, bidding the clueless guard good-bye. *Time to find out what's happening inside.*

Sydney dropped lightly onto a metal catwalk directly below the window. Easing her night vision goggles up onto her forehead, she blinked as her eyes adjusted to the interior light. No longer seeing everything through a luminous green filter, she took in the sights and sounds of the refurbished monastery. Yellow paint protected the catwalk from rust. Heavy machinery hummed, hissed, and gurgled in the background, along with the hubbub of multiple voices. She carefully moved the excised pane of glass away from her feet.

The elevated walkway ran around the upper perimeter of the ex-cathedral, which had been gutted to create a vast space filled with chemical processing equipment. Pipes connected a complicated array of shining steel tanks, pumps, valves, gauges, autoclaves, boilers, and cooling units. Technicians in white lab coats and safety goggles monitored computerized control panels, while a handful of bored-looking thugs guarded the various entrances and exits. Sydney counted only four lab workers; much of the process appeared to be automated, with robotic systems carrying out most of the actual work as mechanical arms collected samples from the various tanks and boilers, then processed them for testing.

Sydney tried to make sense of the setup below. She and Vaughn had taken a tour of a winery in Napa Valley the summer before. There had been plenty of shiny steel tanks and automated apparatuses there as well, but this looked much more elaborate, more like the interior of a nuclear power station—or perhaps a mad scientist's laboratory.

Peering down from the catwalk, she wondered which of the gleaming receptacles contained *meltdown_man*'s bootleg neptunium. *Or has all of the Np-237 been converted into Black Thorine already?*

The diverse pipes converged on a sealed chamber completely enclosed by transparent plastic walls that appeared to be at least six inches thick. Inside the blast-proof room, the varied pipes fed into a single conical mixer. A viscous black liquid oozed out of the bottom of the contraption, slowly working its way down a tall column of spiral tubing into a pressurized metal cylinder about the size of a thirty-five-pound scuba tank. A wheeled robot operated a series of valves attached to the tubing. Judging from the extensive safety precautions, Sydney didn't need Marshall's gamma ray scanner to guess that she had found the Black Thorine.

Now she just needed to get it away from Murnau and his people, preferably without blowing this entire region of Spain to kingdom come. She was only too aware that the bustling town of Sant Sadurní del Noia was only a few miles away, along with assorted neighboring farms and wineries. Sydney suspected that there was enough Black

Thorine here to take out everything for miles around.

But where was Murnau? Was he there in person? From her vantage point upon the catwalk she could only see part of the area below. A forest of pipes and machinery obscured her view of the western end of the vaulted cathedral, so she crept stealthily along the elevated walkway, ducking her head to avoid the hissing steam pipes crossing her path.

Rounding a corner, she stepped onto a long stretch of scaffolding that ran along the northern side of the former cathedral. Once she had worked her way past a vertical support column, she managed to get a good look at the floor area beyond the safety chamber. A trio of figures stood outside the thick plastic walls, watching the Black Thorine flow into the pressurized vessel. Her eyes instantly zoomed in on the man in the middle.

It was Murnau!

An entrance to the wine cellar was located outside the old refectory, where the bygone monks had once taken their meals. Dixon was pleased to discover that this part of the monastery appeared very quiet. The refectory looked dark and deserted; apparently, all the action was happening at the renovated cathedral. Sydney, it seemed, had taken on the more difficult assignment.

Is she up to this? Dixon worried. The murders back home were obviously having an effect on her, impairing her concentration and technique, yet he was reluctant to judge her too harshly. After his wife was murdered, Dixon had gone through a difficult period himself. Sydney had stood by him then, and he intended to do the same for her. *That's what partners are for.*

He approached the entrance via the shadow-cloaked foliage of the vineyards. His night vision goggles alerted him to the presence of a solitary guard posted in front of the cellar doors. The man swept his flashlight about in a desultory fashion while pacing back and forth in front of the closed steel doors. His face held a bored expression, and an open bottle of wine rested in front of the entrance. He clearly wasn't anticipating trouble.

He doesn't look like he'll be much of an obstacle, Dixon thought.

He considered the guard's presence at this

location. Was the man protecting Murnau's stockpile of Black Thorine, or just ensuring that no intruders entered the monastery by means of the catacombs? Either way, Dixon knew that he had to get past the guard if he wanted to search the cellars for the powerful explosive.

The flashlight beam drifted toward Dixon, and he retreated back into the vineyard until it passed. Then he crept back up to the very edge of the field and quietly scooped up a handful of gravel. He hurled the gravel past the guard so that the loose stones fell noisily on the other side of the sentry. The startled guard drew his gun and spun toward the noise, turning his back on Dixon. Eschewing his own pistol, Dixon fired a tranquilizer dart from a concealed compartment in his wristwatch. The small orange missile hit the guard in the back of his neck.

Sometimes the old tricks work best, Dixon thought.

The guard slapped at his neck, as if he had been stung by a bee. His legs wobbled, and Dixon rushed forward to catch him before he could crash to the ground. Grabbing on to the guard beneath his arms, Dixon quietly lowered the unconscious man onto the gravel before confiscating his firearm. Dixon tucked the extra gun into his belt and took the man's flashlight as well.

Now that the guard had been neutralized, Dixon took a closer look at the entrance to the cellar. A pair of rusty iron doors were mounted over a slanted stone hatchway projecting from the base of the refectory wall. A shiny new padlock secured the doors.

He picked the lock in a matter of seconds, then quietly opened the hatch. A flight of worn stone steps led into the catacombs below. Dixon dragged the unconscious guard down the steps and closed the iron doors behind him. He dropped the limp body onto the floor of the cellar, where it landed with a muffled thump.

Dixon assessed his surroundings. This section of the ancient catacombs had indeed been converted into a well-stocked wine cellar. Instead of finding the bones of long-dead monks resting in their sepulchral niches, he saw what appeared to be gallons and gallons of wine stored in both glass bottles and large wooden barrels. On the left side of the cellar, a wrought iron wine rack held row after row of tinted bottles. On the right, four rows of traditional casks were stacked on top of one another, with the circular lids of the barrels facing out. The years of vintage were printed on the exposed lids.

The air within the cellar was cool and dry. Beyond the wine a stone archway led deeper into the gloomy catacombs. Cobwebs stretched across the threshold, suggesting that no one had visited the tunnels in some time. A digital timer, embedded above the archway, looked out of place among the centuries-old architecture. The darkened face of the timer was set at 0:00. Dixon wondered at its purpose.

A slender chain dangled from a naked lightbulb installed in the ceiling. He tugged on the chain to turn on the light, then removed his night vision goggles. The muted earth tones of the cellar displayed their actual colors, free of the unnatural green glow of the goggles. Dixon shrugged off his backpack and rummaged through the equipment inside. A loud snore drew his attention back to the drugged guard lying at the foot of the steps. In theory, the man should be out for hours, but Dixon took a few minutes to bind and gag the sentry with duct tape, just in case.

Once the guard had been dealt with, Dixon

contemplated the assortment of bottles and barrels lined up all around him. He grabbed a bottle at random. A colorful label identified the contents as *cava*, the sparkling champagne for which the Penedès region was best known. He shook his head at the sheer number of potential hiding spots the cellar presented. There had to be at least dozens of bottles of wine in the cellar, not to mention the stacked casks on the other side of the room. Any one of the innocuous containers, he realized, could contain all or some of the Black Thorine Murnau had produced . . . or none at all.

Shades of Notorious, Dixon thought, recalling the classic Hitchcock film in which Cary Grant is forced to search Claude Rains's capacious wine cellar for some stolen uranium. As Dixon recalled, Grant barely finds the right bottle in time. *Too bad I don't have an Ingrid Bergman to help me look.* Sydney no doubt had her own hands full stalking Murnau.

Dixon drew Marshall's gamma ray scanner from the backpack and aimed the sensors at one of the oak barrels. To his disappointment, the detector was even less precise than before. Ironically, the closer the scanner got to the monastery, the more overwhelmed its sensitive circuitry seemed to become. There was no way he could use it to isolate an individual bottle or cask.

Dixon sighed. He would have to do this the hard way—by methodically inspecting each and every container in the cellar. Putting away the useless scanner, he uncorked the nearest bottle and sniffed its mouth. A fruity bouquet greeted his nostrils. It smelled like champagne to him. He poured a sample into his palm. The liquid was a pale golden hue.

It was definitely *cava*. He returned the bottle to its slot and took out the next one.

This was going to take awhile. . . .

Sydney watched Murnau from the catwalk.

The German terrorist was staring intently at the lethal black fluid being decanted into the steel cylinder. He looked exactly as Sydney remembered him, complete with a bushy black unibrow and a handlebar mustache. An open trench coat was draped over his stocky shoulders, and his foot tapped impatiently against the tiled floor.

Murnau was flanked by two associates, neither of whom Sydney recognized. A middle-aged male in a rumpled white lab coat—presumably a scientist—

stood to the left of Der Werwolf, looking distinctly nervous. Coke-bottle glasses rested upon his nose, and a fringe of gray hair ran around the back of his head, giving him the look of a tonsured monk. Mediterranean features suggested that he might be a local. He anxiously dabbed at his brow with a handkerchief while manipulating some sort of remote control device. Sydney guessed that he was in charge of the technical end of the operation. She wondered what had him more worried, Murnau or the Black Thorine? Working for a ruthless terrorist had to be hard on one's nerves.

Then again, I should know—I report to Arvin Sloane.

On Murnau's right was a tall blond Amazon who bore a striking resemblance to the late Kimber Gill. A tight white tank top showed off the bulging biceps and deltoids of a female bodybuilder. Combat boots and hip-hugging black trousers completed her ensemble. Her flaxen hair, tied up in ringlets, fell past her shoulders. More than six feet tall, she towered over both Murnau and the twitchy scientist. A holstered handgun rested against her hip.

Looks like Murnau has a Valkyrie fetish, Sydney surmised. He seemed to prefer female enforcers—

not unlike that biker chick back at Mythos. Syd
eyed the strapping blond woman below. *Wonder if
he's sleeping with this bodyguard too?*

Sydney's hand rested on the grip of her own
pistol. It was tempting to take out Murnau right
here and now; one shot would rid the world of Der
Werwolf forever—and it wouldn't even take a silver
bullet. However, APO would want to thoroughly
interrogate Murnau before "retiring" him, in order
to find out everything they could about his terrorist
network and contacts. That meant taking him alive,
if possible.

She was also reluctant to start firing live ammo
around all the volatile chemicals below. Even with
the Black Thorine contained inside the blast-proof
chamber, a stray shot could easily set off an explosion that might blow them all to bits. While she
wanted to dispose of Murnau and his minions, she
wasn't ready to sacrifice her own life just yet, let
alone turn Dixon's kids into orphans. This wasn't
supposed to be a suicide mission.

Syd crouched down behind the painted
guardrail, doing her best to keep out of sight.
Shrugging out of her backpack, she removed a pen-
size parabolic microphone from the pack. The mic

transmitted on the same frequency as her comms unit, allowing her to eavesdrop on the trio below without the need for a separate earpiece.

"Can't you go any faster?" Murnau snarled in Spanish at the scientist beside him. He glanced at his wristwatch as the Black Thorine sluggishly oozed through the coiled tubing several yards away. "I am not pleased, Dr. Lorca. We are falling far behind schedule."

"Please, Senor Murnau, you have to understand," the scientist pleaded. A Catalan accent gave his Spanish a distinctly nasal quality. He fidgeted nervously with the remote control. "This is a very delicate procedure. We have to proceed carefully, for safety's sake."

Murnau was not appeased. "So you keep saying, but I'm rapidly running out of patience. I expected my Black Thorine to be ready weeks ago." He glowered at the scientist. "You have everything you need here. Perhaps you were the wrong man for the job?"

"No, you mustn't think that!" Lorca insisted anxiously. "It's just that this proved to be a more challenging process than we first anticipated. Obtaining the correct formula was only the first step. We still had to perfect the technique." He backed away from Murnau. "We're almost finished! Look, you can see the Black Thorine right in front of you. All we need is a few more minutes to make sure it's contained properly!"

"Get on with it, then," Murnau groused. "I'm paying you and your people enough."

The imposing blonde said nothing. Apparently, she was the strong, silent type.

"*Sí, sí* . . . of course!" Lorca worked his hand-held gadget as if his life depended on it, which it probably did. "We're almost ready."

Sydney didn't like the sound of that. There was no way was she letting Murnau walk away from here with a tankful of superexplosive. *One way or another, I'm shutting him down.*

In the safety chamber the last of the Black Thorine drained into the containment tank. The remote-controlled robot dutifully sealed off the valves and disconnected the steel cylinder from the mixer. Pincerlike claws took hold of the tank by its handles and lifted it out of its niche beneath the tubing. The robot's torso pivoted 180 degrees so that it faced Murnau and the others, who were waiting right outside the chamber. Carrying the tank in front of it, the

211

robot wheeled toward the exit. Clear plastic doors slid open automatically, allowing the robot to deliver the tank to the trio at the far end of the winery. The blond Valkyrie stepped forward to take possession of the explosive.

"Are you certain that you duplicated the formula precisely?" Murnau asked. "This is truly Black Thorine?"

"Beyond a doubt!" Lorca proclaimed, falling over himself to appease the German. "All our tests confirm that this is the proper compound."

Lucky us, Sydney thought. There was no time to call for reinforcements or try to shadow Murnau back to his lair. If she was going to make a move, it needed to be now.

"Phoenix to Outrigger," she hailed Dixon. "Murnau has the package. I'm going for it."

"Hang on, Phoenix!" he objected. "Wait for me. . . ."

"Sorry, Outrigger. There's no time for that."

She put away the mic and drew her gun instead. Keeping low, she snuck down the length of the catwalk toward the western end of the facility, where the front entrance to the cathedral was located. Perhaps if she took Murnau and the Black Thorine hostage, she could bluff her way past the guards long enough to call for an immediate extraction? With luck, the goons below wouldn't want to risk their boss's life—or set off the superexplosive. Between her and Dixon, they should be able to manage both Murnau and the heavy canister. Maybe they could even force the blonde to carry it for them.

The odds were against her, but what other choice did she have? They were running out of time. Sydney kicked herself for not tracking down the German earlier. Maybe if she hadn't been so distracted by the alias killings she could have discovered the hidden laboratory days earlier. . . .

Which may have been exactly what Murnau had in mind. Anger flared inside her at the thought that Murnau might have contracted the killings of Vicky King and the other women just to throw her off her game. *One more reason to make sure he doesn't get away again,* Sydney thought fiercely. If Murnau *was* behind the murders, she was going to make sure he lived to regret it. *He should never have made this personal. . . .*

Her mind on her suspicions, she failed to notice a screwdriver that some careless worker had left lying on the floor of the catwalk . . . until the tip of her shoe sent the tool clattering noisily across the metal grille.

No! To her horror, Sydney saw the screwdriver roll toward the very edge of the catwalk. She dove for the tool, hoping to grab on to it before it went over the brink, but she was too late. Only inches away from her desperate fingers, the screwdriver rolled under the guardrail and dropped out of sight. It clanged loudly against the lid of a stainless steel tank.

"Damn!" she swore. She didn't need to hear the agitated shouting below to realize that she had just lost the element of surprise. She scrambled back onto her feet, crouching behind the guardrail for cover. "Phoenix to Outrigger. I've been made!"

The wine bottles had contained nothing but wine.

All the Black Thorine must be in the cathedral, Dixon guessed. He had uncorked every bottle, but found only *cava.* Just the same, he wanted to check out the contents of the oak barrels quickly before he left the cellar. *That guard was posted here for a reason.*

A tap had been driven into the lid of one of the

stacked barrels. FALL 2005 read the stamp on the lid. He turned the spigot, expecting champagne to pour onto the floor, but nothing flowed from the tap. Not even a drop of wine landed at his feet.

He frowned. The lack of *cava*, and the deceptive label struck him as ominous. If not champagne, what was being stored in the barrels?

Trusting his instincts, he placed his goggles back on. A miniature reel concealed in the nose-piece yielded a length of fiber-optic cable no more than ten microns in diameter. Dixon knelt in front of the suspicious barrel and carefully threaded the slender glass fiber up through the spigot, into the cask itself. He flicked a switch on the goggles, shifting from night vision to an endoscopic view of the barrel's interior.

His eyes widened at the sight of what looked like several blocks of off-white modeling clay. "Good Lord," he whispered.

He recognized C-4 when he saw it. There was enough plastic explosive in the wine barrel to turn the entire monastery into a smoking crater.

Murnau has this whole place wired to explode.

"Phoenix to Outrigger," Sydney blurted out over the comms, before he even had a chance to alert her to the danger he had just uncovered. "Murnau has the package. I'm going for it."

"Hang on, Phoenix!" he replied anxiously. "Wait for me!"

"Sorry, Outrigger. There's no time for that."

Dixon's heart sped up. He found himself torn between two immediate priorities. Should he go to Sydney's aid first or try to disarm the bomb? For all he knew, there could be more C-4 in the other casks. Velaquez Winery was a death trap that could be triggered at any minute. Withdrawing the optical fiber, Dixon snatched the goggles away from his face. His gaze was drawn to the digital timer above the tunnel entrance. It was still set at 0:00, but now he had a pretty good idea what it was for.

Suddenly he heard footsteps outside the cellar. "Carlos?" a voice called out. "Where the hell are you? There's trouble in the lab!"

Another guard, Dixon guessed. Jumping to his feet, he turned off the light and hid in the shadows next to the steps leading down into the cellar, just as the iron doors were thrown open with a resounding *clang*. A flashlight probed the inky shadows below. Dixon plastered himself against the cool stone wall behind him. He quietly plucked a wine bottle from the rack to his left. His fingers closed around the neck of the bottle as he raised it high above his head.

"Phoenix to Outrigger," Sydney reported. "I've been made!"

Damn, Dixon thought. Things were getting out of hand.

The flashlight beam fell upon Carlos's trussed-up body, which Dixon had not had time to move. *"Caramba!"* the second guard exclaimed from the top of the stairs. He hurried down the steps to check on his comrade.

Dixon swung the bottle like a club. A second later tinted glass shattered against the back of the guard's skull. . . .

Down on the floor of the lab, Murnau was in a rage. "Get that woman!" he shouted. Sydney no longer needed the mic, but she couldn't tell if he had recognized her yet. "After her! *Schnell!*"

"Don't shoot!" Dr. Lorca shrieked at the guards. Panic raised his voice several octaves. "One ricochet could kill us all!"

The blonde barked orders into a cell phone.

Sydney caught a snatch of a Danish accent. "Greta here! Emergency retrieval . . . now!"

Frightened lab workers scurried for cover as Murnau's goons went into action. Footsteps pounded on the metal stairs at both ends of the catwalk, trapping Sydney on her perch. A Spanish-looking guard, moving faster than his cohorts, reached the top of the stairs in seconds. He came charging at Sydney, waving a heavy wrench above his head. "Nosy bitch!" he cursed at her in Catalan. "I'll smash your skull in!"

You can try, she thought. Holding her fire, she watched her attacker's eyes, not his weapon, waiting for the exact moment he took a swing at her. A giveaway look in his eyes alerted her a split second in advance, and she ducked to the left just as the wrench came arcing down at her head. The improvised weapon collided with the top of the guardrail instead, sending a jolt all the way up the thug's arm. He grunted in discomfort, and Sydney took advantage of his momentum to grab on to his legs and tip him over the edge of the rail. A scream trailed behind him as he plummeted forty feet to the floor below. A sickening thud echoed through the winery.

That was one down, but she was still outnumbered eighteen to one. More guards converged on her from both sides. Unlike their overeager compatriot, they advanced cautiously toward her, not wanting to meet the same fate as the first guard. Stained glass splintered beneath the men's boots.

"Give it up, *puta*," said the thug leading the pack on the right. He held out a beefy palm. "Hand over the gun. You're not going anywhere." A gold tooth glittered between his froglike lips. "Don't make us do this the hard way."

Sydney turned her Beretta toward Murnau, but the blonde, Greta, stepped in the way, shielding the German with her well-toned body. Murnau himself blocked the canister of Black Thorine. So much for bluffing her way out of this; Sydney hastily looked around for another option. An insulated steam pipe ran perpendicular to the catwalk, slightly more than a foot above the guard with the gold tooth and the men behind him. Sydney decided to risk a single bullet.

The Beretta's muzzle flared. The gunshot punctured the pipe, tearing open two gaps in the insulation. Hot steam gushed from the vents, scalding the goons. A hissing sound competed with the screams of the guards. The billowing clouds drove the men back, but the hot air came surging toward Sydney as well. *How about that?* she thought, breathing a sigh of relief. *I didn't blow the place up after all.*

She didn't stick around long enough to get burned. Climbing up onto the rail, her actions masked somewhat by the spreading steam, she leaped off the catwalk. Her athletic legs propelled her through the air toward her target: the top of a large cylindrical tank, about thirty feet above the floor of the winery. She touched down nimbly onto the smooth steel surface and grabbed on to a vertical pipe to steady herself. Her black woolen cap came loose, causing her long brown hair to tumble down past her ears. Up on the catwalk, irate guards shouted in confusion. The entire length of the walkway was now thickly shrouded in steam. Angry curses and groans escaped the scalding mist.

But where was Murnau and the Black Thorine?

Peering down from atop the tank, Sydney spotted the terrorist and his associates still standing outside the safety chamber. Murnau's jaw was hanging open, as if he couldn't believe what was happening. He made eye contact with Sydney across the open space above the machinery.

"Bristow!" he growled. Hatred contorted his

hirsute features. Clearly, he had not forgotten Sydney, nor her role in his mistress's death. He yanked a Glock semiautomatic from beneath his lapel and swung it up toward Sydney. "Die, you murdering American slut!"

"Wait!" Dr. Lorca yelped. He grabbed on to Murnau's gun arm and dragged it down. "Are you insane? You'll kill us all!"

Listen to the man, Sydney urged him silently. Although she'd avoided disaster on the catwalk, she didn't want to press her luck by firing at Murnau, especially not while he was standing behind a pressurized tank of Black Thorine. Greta moved quickly to get between Sydney and Murnau once more, just in case Syd decided to take a shot at the German. The bodyguard glared defiantly at Sydney, almost daring her to fire.

"Release me, you worthless imbecile!" Murnau shouted angrily at Lorca. Wresting his arm away from the doctor's grasp, he smacked Lorca viciously across the face with his pistol. The scientist's glasses went flying, and he staggered backward, clutching his nose. Blood streamed through his pudgy fingers as his glasses shattered upon the tiles. "I owe that bitch!"

But before Murnau could take aim at Sydney again, Greta laid a restraining hand upon his arm. "The doctor is right, Oskar!" she said urgently. Keeping one eye on Sydney, she tried to lead Murnau toward the exit. "Let our men handle this!"

Murnau's furious gaze fell on a lab worker standing several feet away, his back pressed up against the southern wall of the winery. "You there," he snarled, gesturing at the pale-faced technician with his Glock. "Drag her down from there!"

"Me?" the techie gulped. Tackling armed intruders was presumably not part of his job description. Video games seemed more his speed. "Are you nuts?"

Murnau aimed the Glock between the young man's eyes. "Do you really want to find out?" He nodded at the looming steel cylinder. "Get her . . . now!"

A ladder ran up the side of the tank currently sheltering Sydney. Looking like he fully expected to be shot at any minute, the techie raced over and started climbing the ladder toward the agent. She thought she heard him reciting a prayer under his breath.

Sydney kicked him in the chin and sent him tumbling backward onto the floor. Murnau sneered in disgust. Sydney heard the real hired muscle stomping down the stairs from the catwalk; the men sounded pissed off and up for a fight. More guards came pouring in from outside the old monastery. "Over there!" their boss bellowed. "She's an American spy. Kill her!"

"Oskar, we have to get out of here!" Greta insisted. She hefted the canister of Black Thorine onto her shoulder and tugged on his collar with her free hand, all the time taking care to stay between Sydney and Murnau. "We have what we came for. Let's go!"

Murnau scowled, but he seemed to get the message. "Lorca!" he barked at the bleeding scientist as he let the blonde hustle him toward the door. "Activate the eradication protocol! Destroy it all!"

"Yes, of course!" Lorca swallowed hard, then rushed over to computer console a few yards away. Deprived of his glasses, he squinted at the monitor as he hesitantly keyed a sequence in the controls. His crumpled nose dripped blood onto the keyboard. "I can't see a damn thing," he muttered.

Sydney saw both Murnau and the Black Thorine getting away from her. Ignoring the ladder, she leaped from the tank onto the roof of the safety chamber, and from there to the floor below. Her legs absorbed the impact, and she hit the ground running. Gripping her Beretta, she chased after Murnau and his flaxen-haired bodyguard. Her heart pounded in her chest.

"Outrigger!" she yelled to Dixon through her comms. "Murnau is bolting. What is your status?"

"I'm still in the cellar," he informed her apologetically. "I had some unwanted company. And, Phoenix, they've got enough C-4 down here to blow this whole place sky-high!"

Terrific, Sydney thought.

A guard lunged into her path, his face boiled red. Aiming low, Sydney shot the man in the foot. He grunted and dropped onto one knee. She shoved him aside and didn't look back. Another thug tried to tackle her, and she knocked him off his feet with a sideways kick to the gut. Every second's delay grated on her nerves. She couldn't let Murnau's goons slow her down.

An emergency siren started wailing loudly, and flashing red lights cast a crimson glow over the chaos. "Eradication protocol initiated," an automated voice announced over a loudspeaker. "Evacuate facility immediately. You have four minutes."

A self-destruct mechanism? Glancing to one side, Sydney spotted Lorca turning away from the computer console. Aside from a dark purple bruise, his face was completely drained of color. His panicked expression confirmed her suspicion, as did the explosives Dixon had just found in the wine cellar. *I guess Murnau doesn't want to leave any evidence behind.*

Panicked guards and technicians abandoned their posts, stampeding past Sydney in a headlong rush for the exits. Suddenly ignored by the fleeing goons, Syd concentrated on catching up with Murnau.

By now the terrorist and his bodyguard were framed in a doorway that led outdoors. Sydney glimpsed the moonlit parking lot beyond, and heard the unmistakable *whump-whump* of an approaching helicopter. Greta's "emergency retrieval," no doubt.

"Freeze, Murnau!" she shouted. "Don't give me another good reason to shoot you!"

"Go ahead!" the blonde retorted. Spinning around to face Sydney, she swung the Black Thorine off her shoulder and held it up in front of her like a shield. "Keep going!" she shouted at Murnau as she backed through the doorway behind him. Along with the vital canister, a handful of disorganized, rushing evacuees blocked the fugitives from Sydney. The copter touched down in the parking lot, its spinning rotors stirring up a cloud of loose dust and gravel. Murnau clambered into the passenger compartment, with Greta trailing behind him. "Wait for me, Oskar!" She yelled. Not that it was necessary—Murnau wouldn't have left without the explosive.

Damn it! Sydney seethed in frustration. She couldn't fire at the helicopter for fear of igniting the Black Thorine. The aircraft took off into the night sky as the ear-piercing siren continued to warn of the winery's imminent destruction. Murnau had escaped . . . again. *And I didn't even get a chance to find out if he was behind the alias killings.*

"Three minutes to eradication," the automated voice announced. "Evacuate immediately."

Sydney scanned the doomed facility, looking

for something to salvage out of this debacle. She spotted Dr. Lorca heading for the exit, clutching an armload of papers. Notes for manufacturing Black Thorine, perhaps?

"Not so fast," she informed him, grabbing on to the scientist by the collar. He tried to break free and she brutally twisted his arm behind his back. Lorca gasped in pain as the loose documents tumbled onto the floor. Sydney barked into his ear. "How do I stop the self-destruct sequence?"

She had failed to capture Murnau, but maybe the deserted facility still held some clue that would lead her to the terrorist's ultimate objective. *If we can keep it in one piece long enough for me to find it.*

"You can't!" Lorca exclaimed. "It's irreversible!" He squirmed frantically in her grasp. "Please, you have to let me go. This whole place is doomed!"

Thanks to the C-4 in the cellar, no doubt, she thought. "You got that, Outrigger?"

"Roger, Phoenix. Just give me a few minutes to try to defuse this situation."

"Go to it!" Sydney replied.

Sydney prodded Lorca forward with the muzzle of her gun. "Okay, doctor, you're coming with me."

Interrogating the scientist was their best lead if Dixon failed to disarm the bomb. "Don't give me any trouble." She suddenly realized that his free hand was digging around in the pocket of his lab coat. "Whoa, there! Get that hand out where I can see it!"

A pair of metallic pincers clamped down on her wrist. *The robot!* she realized instantly. She had forgotten all about it!

The mechanical claw squeezed tightly, eliciting an agonized whimper from Sydney's lips. It pulled her gun arm down, nearly yanking the limb from its socket. Gritting her teeth, she struggled to hold on to the grip of her Beretta despite the pain. Lorca added to her distress by kicking her viciously in the shins until she let go of his arm. He stumbled away from her, clutching the remote control device that must have been in his pocket. Turning around to face her, he squinted at her myopically. Dried blood was caked beneath his nose. A swollen purple bruise distorted his features.

"Who are you, anyway?" His fingers toyed with the remote control. Was he about to command the robot to tear her apart?

"Two minutes to eradication." The prerecorded message reminded Lorca of the coming conflagration. Choosing safety over revenge, he raced out of the winery, leaving Sydney trapped in the robot's manacle-like grip. She tried to slide her hand free of the pincers, but they were clamped too tightly. Unconcerned with its own self-preservation, the immobile robot refused to let go.

"Phoenix to Outrigger. How are you doing on that bomb?"

Dixon's voice was strained. "I haven't given up yet, but you might want get clear of the winery, just in case."

"I'm afraid that's not an option. . . ."

1:58 read the lighted display on the digital timer, which had lit up a few minutes before, at approximately the same time Sydney had reported that the self-destruct sequence had been activated in the cathedral. Dixon didn't need to be a genius of Marshall's order to connect the two events.

One minute and fifty-eight seconds before the C-4 went off.

The cellar reeked of champagne. The waylaid guard lay in a puddle of spilled *cava* and broken glass, not far from his tranquilized associate. Beneath the glow of the naked lightbulb, Dixon briefly wrestled with a moral dilemma: should he waste precious seconds trying to drag the two unconscious men to safety? He had killed before in the line of duty, but he was still hesitant to put the helpless guards at risk of being blown to shreds. The situation raised painful memories of that time, back during his SD-6 days, when he had blown up a laboratory in Germany, not knowing that a CIA tactical team was still inside. Although he had not learned the truth of that incident until years later, after he had joined the CIA, the memory still haunted him. Four good men had died in that explosion. . . .

He glanced at his fallen foes, then reluctantly turned away. Realistically, there was no way he could get them clear of the blast area even if he tried. And Sydney's safety took priority. Better that he attempt to defuse the bomb before it killed them all—and destroyed every last trace of Murnau's operation here.

1:56.

Fortunately, in anticipation of finding the Black Thorine, Dixon had come prepared to defuse a bomb. Reaching into his backpack, he removed a set of mechanical components, including a pressurized container the size of a soda can. He kept one eye on the timer as he quickly assembled a portable bomb disruptor, which resembled the world's most sophisticated Super-Soaker squirt gun. The advanced device worked by blasting an ultrahigh pressure stream of H_2O into a bomb's firing mechanism, blowing apart the detonator's circuitry without igniting the explosive.

At least, that was the theory behind the device. A fully equipped bomb squad would use a remote-controlled robot—not unlike the one now holding Sydney captive—to operate the disruptor, just in case the bomb went off anyway. Dixon didn't have that luxury.

1:49.

The disruptor was ready. Now he just needed to gain access to the firing mechanism inside the barrel. Grabbing on to the spigot with both hands, he strained to wrench the metal tap from the lid of the cask. He kept reminding himself that C-4 was almost impossible to set off without a detonator or blasting cap; it was said you could fire a bullet into the versatile plastic explosive without igniting it. Nevertheless, he held his breath as he struggled with the spigot.

1:45.

The stubborn tap came free at last, exposing an inch-wide hole in the lid. Dixon peered through the gap until he spotted the detonator right where the fiber optics had revealed it earlier. The small black box rested atop the piled blocks of C-4. A tiny red light blinked in synch with the digital timer over the archway, counting down the seconds.

1:43.

He tried to insert the barrel of the disruptor through the hole he had just created. To his frustration, the opening was not quite big enough, and he had to waste precious seconds enlarging the gap with the blade of a Swiss Army knife. By the time he finally got the muzzle through the hole and pressed up against the side of the detonator, he was drenched in sweat. He couldn't help remembering hearing a voice over the comms tell Sydney that the self-destruct sequence was irreversible.

1:25.

His mind flashed back to the last time he had defused a bomb in the field. That had been a close one too, but he had ultimately come through the ordeal in one piece. *Here's hoping history repeats itself.*

He spared a moment to think of his children. *Good-bye, Robin; good-bye, Steven. If I never see you again, always remember that I loved you. . . .*

He braced the stock of the disruptor against his shoulder. His finger tightened on the trigger.

1:20.

There was no time to lose. Offering up a silent prayer, he squeezed the trigger. Compressed water slammed into the detonator, smashing it to pieces. Dixon barely felt the recoil against his shoulder, yet he half-expected the C-4 to obliterate him in a heartbeat. When a second later he found himself still alive and aware, he realized that his odds of surviving the next few seconds had just improved dramatically.

0:37.

He watched tensely as the digital timer continued to tick down to zero. Was there a back up firing mechanism? If so, he was about to find out.

0:00.

Nothing happened. The timer clicked off, but the cellar—as well as the rest of the old monastery—remained as solidly intact as ever. *Irreversible, indeed!*

"Outrigger to Phoenix. The bomb is dead!"

Thank God, Sydney thought, letting out a massive sigh of relief. She was still trapped by the robot, but now she had time to focus on extricating herself from its mechanical clutches. Dixon would arrive in a few minutes, but she didn't feel like waiting for a rescue. The pincers were cutting off the circulation to her fingers, and it was getting more painful by the moment. Besides, she didn't want to take the chance that Lorca or another one of Murnau's flunkies would come back to check on her or the lab before Dixon arrived.

Stretching her neck, she peered back over her shoulder at the stationary robot, taking a closer look at its design. From what she could see, the machine's arms and claws were operated by hydraulics. Her eyes traced a length of rubber tubing connecting the claws to what appeared to be a pump installed in the robot's base. A potential weak spot?

Let's find out, she thought.

Reaching behind her back, she clumsily transferred the Beretta from her trapped right hand to her left. She raised the gun and aimed it over her right shoulder at the tubing she had noticed before. She figured she had made a good educated guess as to where to shoot. It wasn't like she hadn't dealt with hostile robots before; her memory briefly flashed back to the mechanical arm she had battled years before in that laboratory in Russia. *I sent that machine to the scrap pile, and I plan on doing the same to this heap of tin.*

She averted her eyes and squeezed the trigger. Sparks flew as hot lead tore through the robot's arm. Hydraulic fluid sprayed from the ruptured tubing. Sydney felt the arm go limp, and she slid her wrist out from between the loose pincers.

That's better. She massaged her wrist to restore her circulation. Her fingers throbbed as the blood rushed back into them.

Looking around, she found herself alone in the abandoned winery. Even the guard with the wounded foot had been helped out of the building by one of his fellow goons. Lorca and the other lab techs were long gone.

And Murnau is still at large . . . with the Black Thorine.

This is all my fault, she thought bitterly. Guilt weighed down on her. If she hadn't been preoccupied with the alias killings, she might have spotted that stupid screwdriver in time, or maybe even caught up with Murnau before the Black Thorine was ready. Now the crazed terrorist was free to carry out his murderous agenda, whatever that might be.

I screwed up—big time.

"Sydney?" Dixon came running into the winery, gun in hand. He spotted her standing in front of the crippled robot. Hydraulic fluid continued to drip from the machine onto the tiles. "Are you all right?"

She nodded glumly. "Yes, but Murnau's gone. And the explosive."

"I see." Mercifully, he didn't press her for details. He lowered his gun as he ascertained that they were alone. His clothes smelled like champagne. "Now what?"

Sydney looked at the papers strewn across the floor. At least the monastery was still intact. Despite the setbacks, she wasn't about to give up.

"Now we search this place from top to bottom until we find out where Murnau is taking the Black Thorine."

CHAPTER 10

DOWNTOWN LOS ANGELES

"You may be relieved to know," Jack said, "that the lasers and explosive charges were removed years ago."

"Glad to hear it," Vaughn replied. He and Jack made their way down an underground access tunnel beneath the streets of the city. Their footsteps echoed hollowly. Flashlight beams preceded them as they walked along the unlit corridor. Dust motes swirled in the beams and a startled mouse scurried away from the light. The air was stale and musty. As far as Vaughn knew, they were the first people to walk this tunnel in years.

Despite their best efforts, their search for Lewis Fretz had reached a dead end. They had interrogated Marlene Fretz's neighbors at the run-down apartment complex, but not one of them had reported seeing any visitors matching Fretz's description. His parole officer and former associates had proved equally unhelpful. No one seemed to have laid eyes on the man for months. Nor had Jack or Vaughn found a Harley-Davidson parked anywhere near the 'Acienda Arms.

That left them with only one last avenue to explore. Reaching into his pocket, Vaughn retrieved one of the business cards Marlene Fretz had shown them. He glanced once more at the obsolete Credit Dauphine logo inscribed upon the card, which had provided the impetus for tonight's expedition. If Fretz was indeed obsessed with his old job and life, perhaps he had felt compelled to return to the site of his glory days?

It was a long shot, but they were running out of options. Sydney was still overseas, and Vaughn remained determined to capture the alias killer before she returned. Nadia and Weiss were focusing on trying to keep any potential victims alive, while the rest of APO's resources were still devoted to the ongoing Murnau situation. Even Vaughn and Jack had been forced to put off this trip until after business hours. By the time Sloane had finally dismissed them for the night, it had been several hours after Sydney's unsuccessful raid on the Spanish winery.

Poor Syd! Vaughn thought. He knew that she had to be beating herself up for letting Murnau get away with the Black Thorine. Sloane had been less than pleased with the outcome of the operation as well. Vaughn was just glad that she and Dixon had managed to get out of that rigged monastery alive; he'd had a few tense minutes monitoring the raid over the comms.

He yawned. Working double shifts every day was taking its toll. He wondered how Jack was coping with all these late nights, especially after his recent bout of radiation poisoning. Only a few weeks before he had needed a cane to get around.

"Bored, Agent Vaughn?" Jack treated his colleague to a withering look. "My apologies if hunting for my daughter's stalker strikes you as tiresome."

Vaughn repressed a sigh. Clearly, Jack's brush with mortality had done little to mellow him. Not for the first time, the younger man wondered what he would be getting into if he proposed to Sydney. Did he really want Jack Bristow as a father-in-law? That was an intimidating prospect, to say the least. And then there was her mother's side of the family. . . .

Sydney is worth it, he reminded himself, just as he always did. *Derevkos and all.*

"I'm fine," he answered. "Let's just get on with this."

They came to what appeared to be a solid concrete wall, blocking their path. A dust-covered fire detector was mounted on the wall. Jack tugged on the circular device and it swung outward, exposing a keypad and a card slot underneath. He removed a blank white card from his wallet and inserted it into the slot. The electronic keypad lit up in response.

"Does Sloane know you have that card?" Vaughn asked.

"Hardly," Jack replied. This excursion was being conducted without Sloane's knowledge or approval. "I have my own connections at the CIA."

Jack typed a six-digit code into the keypad, then stepped back from the wall. Hidden motors thrummed to life, and the wall retracted into the ceiling, exposing an open space beyond. Squeaking gears testified as to how long the concealed machinery had been dormant.

"Welcome to SD-6," Jack said. "Sublevel 6, to be exact."

The old Credit Dauphine building had long since been sold to a legitimate private business, but the subbasements that had once housed SD-6's secret headquarters had been sealed off by the CIA for security purposes. Although an Agency cleanup crew had supposedly stripped the place of any valuable assets or classified technology, the Feds still didn't want any nosy reporters snooping around the site and asking inconvenient questions, especially when those questions might compromise the effectiveness of APO. The elevators in the building above no longer descended to this level. Fortunately, Jack remained familiar with all of the base's hidden escape tunnels.

Vaughn swept the area with his flashlight as they entered the abandoned offices. Not much of the formerly high-tech headquarters remained. Empty desks and overturned chairs gathered dust beneath hanging fluorescent lamps with missing or shattered bulbs. Bullet holes riddled the walls, although someone seemed to have removed any fallen shells or cartridges. The glass doors leading to Sloane's former office were cracked and pockmarked. Cobwebs hung from the ceiling, and rat droppings littered the desks and the floor. The musty air smelled of decay.

Pretty bleak, Vaughn thought. Time and neglect had really done a number on this place. He couldn't help remembering the last time he had set foot in there, the day Sydney had led a CIA commando team to take down SD-6 once and for all. In the thrill of that victory, he and Syd had shared their very first kiss.

He glanced at Jack. Unlike Vaughn, the elder Bristow had worked out of these offices for years— and had nearly died here on more than one occasion. "This must be weird for you," Vaughn commented.

"Nostalgia isn't one of my vices," Jack said coolly. His face betrayed not a trace of emotion as he surveyed the desolate ruins.

Yeah, right, Vaughn thought. He didn't entirely buy the other man's stoic ice man routine, but if that was how Jack wanted to play it, Vaughn wasn't going to challenge him. "Where did Fretz used to work?"

"This way," Jack said. He led Vaughn deeper into the murky subbasement. He swung his flashlight like a machete as he cleared away the cobwebs in their path.

The general air of abandonment discouraged Vaughn. It was hard to imagine that anyone, including Lewis Fretz, would ever want to come back here. There seemed to be little evidence that Fretz had ever returned to his old haunts. *We're wasting our time here.*

Walking past the central bull pen, they turned down a side corridor lined with empty cubicles. A ghastly stench assailed Vaughn's nostrils, forcing him to place a hand over his nose and mouth. He recognized the sickly odor of putrefaction.

"Oh my God," he muttered.

Even Jack seemed put off by the foul smell. Grimacing in distaste, he covered his lower face with a handkerchief as he hurried toward a cubicle near the end. Vaughn followed after him, gagging on the stench, which grew noticeably stronger as he approached the cubicle.

Vaughn had smelled rotting bodies before. He had a pretty good idea of what to expect.

He stepped past the flimsy divider blocking his

view of the cubicle. His eyes widened as he located the source of the odor.

A dead body was slumped over a desk, in front of a laptop. There was a bullet hole through his head and a cold pistol in one hand. Dried blood splattered the desk and wall, while a nauseating mixture of bodily fluids had congealed beneath the corpse's chair, leaving a dark black stain on the tiled floor. Dust and cobwebs coated the body. All signs pointed to suicide.

"Meet Lewis Fretz," Jack said through his handkerchief.

Vaughn was impressed that Jack could still recognize his former coworker. The body was in an advanced state of decay. Most of the flesh had been eaten away, leaving little more than a desiccated husk behind. Dried hair and sinew clung to a skeletal frame. If this was Fretz, he had obviously been dead for weeks.

Which meant there was no way he could be the alias killer.

"Are you certain?" Vaughn asked. The rotting corpse certainly matched Fretz's general description. Wire-frame glasses hung askew from what was left of one ear. Buck teeth protruded from the skeletal jaw. "This was his cubicle?"

Jack nodded. "We'll need to check dental records and DNA to make a positive ID, but I feel confident this is Fretz." He pointed to a framed wedding photo sitting on the desk. Younger versions of Lewis and Marlene smiled at them from happier days. "We've been set up."

It definitely looked that way. Vaughn realized that someone else must have mailed those newspaper clippings to Marlene Fretz. *Just to keep us looking in the wrong direction.*

Lewis Fretz was merely a convenient patsy, and a dead one, to boot.

"What about the computer?" Vaughn asked. He examined the grisly tableau inside the cubicle. Fretz appeared to have been working on the laptop right before he killed himself. Looking more closely, Vaughn saw that the computer was plugged into an outlet beneath the desk. *He must have managed to tap into the building's power somehow.*

"Be my guest," Jack said, stepping aside. Like most Americans of his generation, he preferred to let the younger set deal with any heavy lifting, computer-wise.

"Give me one second." Vaughn eased the laptop

away from Fretz's dead hands, trying to disturb the crime scene as little as possible. The motion jarred the corpse, which started to topple off the chair, but Jack calmly reached out and steadied the body. Maggots and a loose tuft of hair fell to the floor. "Thanks," Vaughn murmured.

The screen saver on the dusty monitor evaporated as Vaughn tapped on the keyboard. An e-mail program appeared on the screen. *This looks promising,* he thought. It took him only a moment to call up the last e-mail Lewis Fretz ever sent:

Marlene,

    I am writing this note to let you know that you never need to worry about me again. By the time you read this, I will have left this wretched world behind. Please know that I never meant for any of this to happen. We both know whose fault this really is.

    I was just a pawn in an insane game, callously sacrificed by people I thought I trusted. But they won't be able to persecute me anymore. Can they still sleep at night, after what they did to me? I know that this is the only way I will ever be able to rest in peace once more.

Please don't feel sorry for me. I want you to move on and get a fresh start. When you think of me in the years to come, try to remember the good times we knew . . . before I was betrayed.

I can't wait any longer. I just want this all to be over. Good-bye, my love.

Yours forever,

Lew

"Take a look at this," Vaughn said. He spun the laptop around so that Jack could read the missive on the screen. "According to the program, he sent this e-mail on March 29th. Weeks before the first murder."

Jack's expression darkened as he perused the electronic suicide note. "You're certain he sent this to Marlene?"

"I believe so," Vaughan answered. "There's no record of the e-mail being bounced back. Marshall should be able to verify that once we get this laptop over to APO."

But if Marlene Fretz knew that her ex-husband

was dead, why didn't she mention that to us? Why would she pretend that she thought those letters were from Lewis?

"Are you thinking what I'm thinking?" he asked Jack.

"I'm afraid so," Jack said. The senior Bristow was visibly troubled. "Let's go."

ATLANTIC OCEAN

The private jet had left Barcelona an hour before.

"I don't get it," Sydney said. "Why the Canary Islands?"

She and Dixon had the passenger cabin to themselves. They sat across from each other in cushioned seats with plenty of legroom. A topographical map of La Palma, one of the Canary Islands off the coast of West Africa, was spread out on a low table between them. Bottled water and a plate of toasted bagels provided an early-morning snack.

They had found the map in an executive office at the old monastery, sitting atop a stack of discarded papers intended for the shredder. *We may not have captured Murnau,* Sydney consoled herself, *but at least we managed to keep him from blowing all the evidence sky-high. And before his people had a chance to clean up after him.*

"I have no idea," Dixon confessed. He had changed out of his wine-soaked fatigues, into fresh civilian attire. Sydney had traded her own fatigues for a sweater and jeans. "Murnau's agenda is virulently anti-American, yet the U.S. has no vital interests on La Palma. We don't even have a consulate there."

Sydney stared at the confiscated map for the umpteenth time, still not seeing any clues to Murnau's endgame. Less than three hundred square miles in area, La Palma was shaped like an upside-down arrowhead, with its jagged tip pointing south. A volcanic ridge ran down the center of the island, while various small towns and villages dotted its coasts. No markings indicated Murnau's ultimate destination. Now that he had his Black Thorine, what possible reason could he have for researching La Palma? The mountainous green island, which was under Spanish jurisdiction, boasted a world-class observatory, but that hardly struck her as a prime target for terrorism. Why waste Black Thorine on a place like La Palma? It wasn't even the most touristy island of the Canaries.

She took out her cell phone and dialed Marshall. Glancing at her watch, she calculated that it was about 8:00 P.M. back home.

"Hello?" Marshall's face appeared on her phone's video screen. She caught a glimpse of his kitchen behind him. "Oh. Hi, Sydney. What's up?"

"Hi back," she replied. "Sorry to bother you at home. Is Carrie around?"

Marshall's wife, an NSA employee, was unaware of his involvement with APO, which meant that a degree of discretion was required whenever his loved ones were in earshot. Sydney knew that Marshall hated having to lie to Carrie about his work, but that was part of the job. She remembered having to do the same with Will and Francie, back when she still had friends who weren't spies.

"Nope," he informed her. "She's attending her Mensa book club meeting tonight. They're poking holes in the new Stephen Hawking book this month. She's been looking forward to it all week." He shrugged. "It's just me and little Mitchell tonight. Kind of a boys' night in." His eyes widened, distracted by something offscreen. "Mitchell, put that down! That is *not* a toy!"

A loud crash resounded in the background. Sydney winced. "Is this a bad time?"

"Just the terrible twos," he said with a sigh. "What can I do for you?"

Sydney wanted to keep this call short, for Marshall's sake. "Have you had a chance to check out La Palma yet?" She had updated Marshall on her discovery earlier, while she and Dixon had been en route to the airport. "Any thoughts regarding Murnau's potential target?"

"No luck so far," he confessed. "I tasked some satellites to scan La Palma, but they didn't show anything that would be considered suspicious. No terrorist bases, top-secret military installations, or anything cool like that. If Murnau is running some sort of operation there, he's keeping it small and out of sight." His eyes nervously tracked an offscreen toddler. "Granted, there are plenty of dense forests to hide in. Did you know that La Palma is also known as La Isla Bonita, 'The Beautiful Island'? That's because there's so much lush vegetation on the island. Ferns and laurel forests, mostly, along with—*Mitchell, stay away from that!*"

Another crash interrupted Marshall's spiel. "Why don't I let you go?" Sydney suggested tactfully. "I'll be in touch if we come up with any new info."

"Sure. Right." Marshall's mind was obviously elsewhere, perhaps wondering how he was going to explain the mess his son had made to his wife later. "Don't be afraid to call if you need something. And good luck!"

"You, too." She suspected Marshall was going to need some luck once Carrie saw the aftermath of his babysitting. "Talk to you later."

She ended the call and put away her phone. "Marshall's just as stumped by this La Palma business as we are," she told Dixon.

"So I heard." He glanced at his watch; it was five in the morning, local time. "We've got another five hours before we reach the Canaries. We ought to try to get some rest." He settled back into his seat and closed his eyes. "Perhaps the answer will come to us in our sleep."

"Sounds like a plan," she agreed. She didn't have any better ideas.

She leaned her head back against the cushions, but sleep eluded her. Although she had trained herself to take advantage of opportunities to nap whenever they presented themselves, this time she had far too much on her mind to drift off into slumber. Her brain kept replaying the raid on the monastery, looking for ways she could have done things better, even as she kept trying to anticipate Murnau's next move. Opening her eyes, she glanced out the window to her right. The first rosy tinges of dawn were beginning to light up the sky. Above the fleecy clouds, the fading moon was almost full. *We're running out of time,* she realized. Whatever Der Werwolf had in mind, it could take place as soon as this coming evening. He had the Black Thorine now. Was he simply waiting for the full moon to rise?

As she pondered Murnau's plan, another part of her mind remained back in Los Angeles. Dawn was still hours away there. For all she knew, the alias killer was about to strike again. . . .

CHAPTER 11

HOLLYWOOD BOULEVARD
LOS ANGELES

Mann's Chinese Theatre was lit up like a Christmas ornament in striking shades of red and green. The world-famous movie palace was a vision of Oriental splendor, its ornate exterior resembling a traditional pagoda, albeit more fanciful than most. Towering coral red columns, adorned with elaborate wrought iron Chinese masks, flanked the entrance, which was guarded by pair of imported stone Heaven Dogs. A thirty-foot-high dragon was carved in stone between the columns. Copper-topped turrets rose from the jade green roof. Dramatic lighting added to the effect.

There were no red-carpet premieres on this particular night, so tourists were free to swarm the theater's fabled forecourt, where they oohed and aahed over the cement footprints of past and present Hollywood stars. The shrines to movie legends continued on the busy sidewalk in front of the theater, where bronze stars embedded in marble plaques honored assorted showbiz luminaries. Avid film fans trod the Hollywood Walk of Fame, reading out loud the names of their favorite celebrities. Local entrepreneurs hawked maps to the stars' homes.

Breakdancers performed for the tourists, along with struggling actors and actresses dressed up as everyone from Charlie Chaplin to Cookie Monster. The self-employed characters posed for snapshots with grinning sightseers, then hit up those same tourists for cash. An energetic impersonator, such as Abella Bernier, could make up to four hundred dollars a night in tips.

A funny way to make a living, Eric Weiss thought, *but I guess you gotta do what you gotta do.* For an aspiring movie star like Abella, those tips probably made the difference between starvation and another day in pursuit of her big break. *I suppose it beats waiting tables. . . .*

Abella Bernier was the next name on the killer's hit list. It was an alias that Sydney had once used while posing as a cabaret singer in Paris. As it happened, there was only one woman by that name living in the L.A. area, so Weiss and Nadia felt confident that they knew who the murderer's next target was.

A lucky break for us, he mused, *if not for Abella.*

He watched the colorful scene from behind a hot dog stand several yards away. Business was slow, exactly as planned. In fact, the wieners broiling on his grill had been chemically concocted, according to Marshall's own secret recipe, to be as unappetizing as possible. Besides having a faintly slimy appearance, each wiener emitted an artificial pheromone that acted as a subliminal appetite suppressant, thus guaranteeing that Weiss, in his alias as a street vendor, would not be distracted from his surveillance duties by a steady stream of customers. So far the doctored dogs were working like a charm; Weiss hadn't sold a hot dog all evening.

He flipped the noxious wieners while keeping a close eye on the front of the theater. Although he avoided looking at her directly, one figure in particular held his attention: an attractive young woman dressed in a spandex superhero costume. The silver outfit clung to the woman's athletic figure. Her gloves, boots, belt, mask, and cape were a bright golden hue, as was the star emblazoned on her chest. A jeweled tiara rested atop her mane of waist-length scarlet hair. All in all, she was the spitting image (or at least a reasonable facsimile) of Quasar Queen herself.

Weiss watched with interest as the costumed woman posed with two beaming schoolkids while their parents took a picture, making sure to get the brightly lit pagoda in the background. Afterward, the busy superheroine waved good-bye before sticking a five-dollar bill into a secret compartment in her accessory belt. "Abella Bernier" seemed to be having a good night.

"Houdini to Evergreen," he whispered into his comms. "Oops, I mean, Quasar Queen."

"Very funny," Nadia replied. She held her cape up in front of her face to conceal her lips. The brilliant red wig and golden mask rendered her unrecognizable. "I can't believe I'm doing this. Why couldn't the real Abella have been an orthodontist or an insurance agent?"

"Hey, this was your idea," he reminded her.

Nadia had insisted on taking the real Abella's place. Posing as FBI agents, they had convinced the struggling actress to go into hiding by telling her that they were tracking a serial killer who was stalking women who shared the same names as his hated ex-girlfriends. As cover stories went, this was close enough to the truth to be convincing. The actual Abella was currently enjoying the hospitality of an APO safe house while Nadia pounded the pavement dressed in silver spandex.

To be honest, Weiss was not thrilled that his girl-friend was essentially placing herself in the killer's sights, but Nadia was dead set on using herself as bait. Nadia had even moved into Abella's dingy apartment in hopes of luring the killer out of hiding. "I don't want another Victoria King on my con-science," she had told him earlier. "I've accepted a life of danger. Abella and these other women haven't done anything to deserve this kind of jeopardy. It's better that I take the risk instead."

Weiss understood where she was coming from, but that didn't mean he had to like it.

"I know this was my idea. Don't remind me," she told him, striking another dramatic pose behind her cape. "Any sign of our target?"

"You mean your diabolical archenemy?" he teased. "Seriously, in this mob, who can tell?" He scanned the crowded sidewalk, looking in vain for the dark-skinned biker chick from the other night. It bothered him that the alias killer could already be there, possibly even disguised as one of the other costumed characters, and he might not be able to recognize her. As much he wanted to catch the murderer, he found himself secretly hoping that she would be a no-show tonight. For Nadia's sake.

Sorry, Syd. I know you're counting on us to nab this psycho.

"So how's the life of a superheroine?" he asked, trying to keep the mood light.

"Not bad." She executed an elegant twirl with her cape, garnering a round of applause. "It's barely past eight and I've already made one hundred and twenty dollars. My butt, on the other hand, is getting pinched within an inch of its life. Damn teenagers." Her voice held a trace of her deadly mother's ferocity. "I've been tempted to break a few fingers, but I don't want to scare the killer off."

That would be a bad thing? Weiss wondered

which of them was more uneasy about the night's perilous operation. *Me, probably.*

"Well, don't worry," he told her, feigning a confidence he didn't feel. "I'm on the lookout."

"Copy that, Houdini. And thanks. I can't think of anyone else I'd rather have watching my back. Quasar Queen out."

Potential customers glanced at the greasy hot dogs, then hurriedly moved on, leaving Weiss free to continue his stakeout. Opening his cash box, he peeked at the photo of Lewis Fretz taped to the inside of the lid to refresh his memory of the man's face. Vaughn had quietly shared Jack's theory regarding Fretz with Weiss back at the office, so Weiss was scanning the crowd for the missing man as well as for the biker chick from Mythos.

No sign of either so far.

Wonder how Vaughn and Jack are doing tonight? Weiss knew that the two men were planning to search SD-6's former headquarters that evening. In fact, they were probably there right now. He silently wished them luck. In an ideal world, Jack and Vaughn would track down the killer before he or she could come after Nadia. *That works for me.*

He tensed as a Marilyn Monroe impersonator, in her iconic *Seven Year Itch* dress, approached Nadia from behind. "Look sharp, Evergreen," he alerted her. "Right behind you!"

Nadia twirled around to face Marilyn, but the other woman appeared to be unarmed. "Excuse me," she said in a breathy approximation of the real Marilyn's voice. "Do you have change for a twenty?"

Weiss relaxed and let out a sigh of relief. This was going to be a long night.

He glanced at the movie marquee overlooking the sidewalk. A new romantic comedy starring Ethan Hawke and Jennifer Lopez was playing inside. The last showing let out a little after midnight; according to the real Abella, that was when she usually called it a night. *Four more hours to go,* he calculated. He wondered if his nerves could take it. He could practically feel himself losing a layer of stomach lining with each passing moment.

Plus, the fumes from the evil wieners were making him kind of queasy. Maybe Marshall needed to tone down the formula a little. . . .

The roar of a motorcycle cut through the hubbub along the boulevard. Weiss looked up to see a familiar-looking Harley-Davidson zooming down the street toward the theater. A figure in a black leather jacket and motorcycle helmet leaned back in the seat as the Harley pulled a wheelie, lifting its front tire high into the air. Visions of a drive-by shooting flashed through Weiss's brain. "Evergreen, watch out!"

The Harley shot past him and Weiss remembered chasing the speeding bike down Santa Monica Boulevard only days earlier. The mystery biker had lost him at the freeway off-ramp then, but he was ready for her now. The body of his hot dog stand contained a microwave vehicle stopper similar to the one Dixon had used in Wilmington. He took aim at the motorcycle and fired the gadget.

The first zap missed the Harley, nailing a convertible instead.

"What the hell?!" the driver exclaimed as his car abruptly slowed to a halt.

Weiss was already taking a second shot at the Harley, which was now only a few yards away from Nadia and the other costumed characters. Weiss's heart was pounding. He knew he had to make this shot count.

That's not just a victim, that's my girlfriend, he thought angrily. *No way is she taking a bullet on my watch!*

He fired the zapper again.

Bingo! A fresh burst of microwaves fried every microchip in the Harley's controls. The biker lost control of the vehicle as the Harley abruptly lost power. The bike skidded across the road, throwing up sparks as its fender and mufflers scraped against the pavement.

Weiss didn't wait for the motorcycle to come to a complete halt. Bolting from behind his hot dog stand, he ran out in front of the stalled convertible and into the street. Horns honked and brakes squealed, but Weiss didn't care that he was blocking traffic. Reaching the Harley in a matter of moments, he dragged the stunned motorcyclist off the bike and hurled the biker roughly onto the pavement. "Freeze!" he shouted, drawing his gun from beneath his greasy vendor's apron. "Don't move a muscle!"

"Okay! Okay!" the biker squealed. "Don't go ballistic on me, dude!"

Huh? Weiss yanked the helmet off the biker's head. Instead of the dark-skinned woman described by both Nadia and Sydney, the man on the ground was a scruffy-looking white teenager with acne and a patchy goatee.

Another false alarm?

Groaning, the kid lifted his head from the pavement. His eyes widened at the sight of the gun aimed at his head. "Whoa!" he exclaimed, throwing his hands up into the air. "I didn't do anything, I swear. It was all that chick's idea!"

"Chick? What chick?" Weiss demanded. He grabbed the kid by the collar and waved the gun in his face.

The teenager couldn't explain fast enough. "This foxy-looking older chick. She said I could keep the bike if I hightailed it down Hollywood Boulevard. She even gave me this helmet and jacket to wear." He gulped as he stared down the barrel of Weiss's gun. "I figured it was some sort of reality show stunt."

Weiss let go of the clueless kid. The Harley was a diversionary tactic, he realized, intended to flush Abella's bodyguards out of hiding. And he had fallen for it.

"Oh no," he whispered. Turning his back on the teenage decoy, he charged back toward the theater, gun in hand. A chill ran down his spine as it dawned on him that he was probably already too late.

The real killer must be after Nadia right now!

HACIENDA ARMS
SAN FERNANDO VALLEY

Search warrants be damned. Jack picked the lock on Marlene Fretz's front door. Gun in hand, he barged into the darkened apartment, with Vaughn following close behind him. "Ms. Fretz?" he called out. "Show yourself!"

No one answered.

"I don't think she's here," Vaughn said. He switched on the lights and closed the door. His Beretta was drawn and ready.

"Thank you, Agent Vaughn," Jack said drily. "I can see that."

Jack kept his gun drawn as he surveyed the silent apartment. The threadbare furnishings provided further evidence of Marlene's reduced circumstances. A ratty sofa that looked like it had been rescued from a thrift store was patched with strips of electrical tape. A small television set rested atop a blue plastic milk carton. A cheap bookcase leaned against one wall, its shelves sagging beneath stacks of paperbacks and magazines. An aluminum foil tray that still held the unappetizing remains of a TV dinner lay forgotten on the fraying orange carpet, which was worn clear through in places. An ashtray on an end table was overflowing with discarded cigarette butts. The room smelled of tobacco and nicotine.

To Jack's mind, the run-down apartment looked only slightly more habitable than the abandoned subbasement he and Vaughn had just left. They had come straight here from SD-6's old headquarters, driven by a growing suspicion that Marlene Fretz had a lot to answer for.

We could still be wrong about her, Jack thought. *But I seriously doubt it.*

"Jack, take a look at this," Vaughn said, calling him over to the bookcase where Marlene had arranged various photos and mementos. Jack recognized the wedding photo they had just found in Lewis Fretz's bloodstained cubicle, but he was surprised to see another photo, this one of Marlene in an Army Rangers uniform, posing with several other soldiers at what looked like Fort Benning. On the same shelf, only a few inches away, a bronze medal testified that Marlene had served in the armed forces during the campaign in Kosovo.

"Did you know that Marlene served in the military?" Vaughn asked him.

"No," Jack said grimly. He silently cursed himself for not researching Marlene's background more carefully. *I knew everything there was to know about the husband, but not nearly enough about the wife.* "And not just the military, but special ops."

Vaughn didn't need any help figuring out the implications of his discovery. "So she would have been trained in hand to hand combat."

"Presumably," Jack agreed. Certain scenarios were looking more and more likely. "We need to search the rest of this place . . . and quickly." With luck, none of Marlene's neighbors had spotted them breaking into the apartment, but he knew it would be unwise to assume that had been the case. They needed to be out of there before the LAPD came by to investigate. "You start with the bedroom. I'll check out the bathroom."

Jack warily entered the bathroom and drew back the shower curtain. After ascertaining that neither Marlene nor anyone else was lurking inside, he started combing through the medicine cabinet and drawers. It didn't take him long to find more incriminating evidence.

A glossy black wig rested in a drawer beneath the sink, along with a tube of light brown grease-paint, contact lenses, lifts, and other makeup and cosmetic supplies. Jack instantly thought of the dark-skinned, black-haired woman Sydney had glimpsed at that nightclub—the stranger who had stabbed Victoria King to death. Apparently that hadn't been Lewis Fretz in disguise. . . .

"Jack! Get in here!" Vaughn called urgently from the bedroom.

He hurried to join the younger man.

Marlene's bedroom was a mess, with discarded articles of clothing strewn about the floor. Housekeeping was low on Marlene's list of priorities, it seemed. Jack was not surprised by the squalor; he was pretty sure that Marlene had other things on her mind.

Papers and photos were spread out on top of her unmade bed. Glancing down, Jack saw file folders and loose documents stacked atop the rumpled sheets. Vaughn was hurriedly leafing through a folder. There was an agitated look upon his face.

"It's all here!" he said. "Sydney's SD-6 files, a complete list of her old aliases, addresses and phone numbers for the victims, even torn pages from the L.A. phone book with the women's names circled." He shook his head.

Jack picked up a folder from the bed and started flipping through it. Inside were surveillance photos of various young women who had obviously been stalked and studied for some time before the killer made her move. Large red *X*s had been drawn across most of the photos with a marker; the exception was a Polaroid of a woman dressed up as some sort of ridiculous comic book character.

Abella Bernier, Jack guessed. Weiss had discreetly kept him up to date on his and Nadia's efforts to protect the remaining targets. Jack was glad to see that Ms. Bernier had not been X-ed out. *Not yet, at least.*

The final photo was the most ominous: an eight by ten glossy of Sydney herself.

"It looks like we've found our culprit," Vaughn said.

"Indeed." Jack told Vaughn about the wig and makeup he had found in the bathroom. "The conclusion is obvious."

Marlene Fretz was the alias killer.

"She must have mailed those newspaper clippings to herself," Vaughn surmised, "in order to divert suspicion onto Lewis instead." He glanced around at the tawdry apartment building. "She must have spent every last cent on her revenge."

Jack remembered bribing Marlene into talking the other night. Had his own funds helped subsidize the woman's insane vendetta? "She obviously blames Sydney for her ex-husband's downfall. I imagine Lewis must have subjected her to his paranoid tirades regarding Sydney's role in betraying SD-6."

"Never mind that it was Sloane and SD-6 that truly duped Lewis," Vaughn said bitterly. "He probably never accepted that he was working for the bad guys his entire career. And now Marlene has bought into that whole scenario."

"And cast Sydney in the role of Benedict Arnold." Jack returned his daughter's photo to the bottom of the stack. He gazed with concern at the snapshot of Abella Bernier in her absurd superhero costume. Nadia, he recalled, was impersonating Abella that very night, over on Hollywood Boulevard.

But where was Marlene Fretz?

"Well, we've zeroed in on the killer at last," Vaughn observed. He gestured toward the reams of damning evidence upon the bed. "Like I said, it's all here. Everything."

"No," Jack corrected him. "One item is missing."

Vaughn gave him a puzzled look. "What's that?"

"The knife that killed Victoria King."

CHAPTER 12

HOLLYWOOD BOULEVARD

"Thanks, Quasar Queen!"

Nadia signed the little girl's autograph book and handed it back to her. The child's excited grin was hard to resist and made tonight's operation a bit more bearable, crazy costume and all. She wondered if the real Abella Bernier still got a kick out of impersonating a superhero every night. *It's kind of like playing Santa Claus,* she thought.

"Evergreen, watch out!"

Weiss's voice blared in her ear, only seconds before she heard the roar of a powerful motorcycle speeding toward her. She looked around the crowded forecourt in alarm; there were dozens of innocent bystanders in front of the theater. Someone was bound to get injured, maybe even killed, if the alias killer started shooting at her.

Please, Eric! Don't give her the chance to hurt someone!

Standing on her toes to peer over the crowd, she was relieved to see a suspicious Harley-Davidson go skidding across the boulevard. Marshall's car zapper must have worked. She watched as Weiss ran out into traffic to confront the downed biker, who appeared to offer no resistance. She considered dashing to her boyfriend's assistance, but it looked like he had the situation under control. Perhaps there was no need to blow her cover.

Thank God, she thought. Maybe this entire nightmare was finally over. She couldn't wait to tell Sydney that they had apprehended the alias killer.

Or had they? Her mind flashed back to that terrible night at Mythos, when the assassin had distracted her and Sydney with a phone call right before killing Vicky King. What if the killer was pulling a similar stunt now?

Growing up in the mean streets of Buenos Aires, Nadia had developed a keen sense for knowing when she was in danger, and she had learned to trust those instincts. A prickling sensation at the back of her neck put her on guard, and she spun around just in time to see a female tourist lunging at her from behind. A crystal blade glittered in the woman's hand.

Nadia jumped backward, barely evading the knife thrust. She kicked out with her right leg, hoping to dislodge the knife from her assailant's hand, but the other woman expertly blocked the kick with her left forearm. *This is no amateur,* Nadia realized. *She's had combat training.*

The woman wore the universal uniform of an American tourist: baseball cap, shorts, sneakers, and a souvenir T-shirt. DISNEYLAND 2005 read the inscription across the woman's chest, above a cartoon drawing of Sleeping Beauty's Castle. Stringy brown hair peeked out from beneath the woman's bright red cap. Her sallow skin looked considerably lighter than it had at Mythos four nights earlier, assuming this was the same woman. Nadia guessed that it was; APO hardly had a monopoly on clever disguises.

It certainly looked like the same knife. Nadia's gaze was irresistibly drawn to the polished quartz weapon in the killer's hand. The six-inch, triple-edged blade was more than capable of delivering a fatal wound. The woman held the knife hammer-style, with the blade jutting upward from her closed fist. The grip was ideal for both slashing and stabbing, not that Nadia intended to give the woman a chance to do either.

"Houdini, Evergreen!" Vaughn's voice unexpectedly came over the comms. "This is Shotgun. We've just learned that the killer is Marlene Fretz. Repeat, the killer is Marlene Fretz. She's on the loose . . . and very dangerous!"

You're telling me, Nadia thought.

At Mythos the killer's attack had set off a panic, but not here. Instead of fleeing, the mob of sightseers cheered and snapped photos, thinking that the fight was an act put on for their entertainment. "Get her, Quasar Queen!" one bystander yelled enthusiastically. More tourists came running into the forecourt to get a better look. "All right!" a teenage boy exclaimed. "Catfight!"

Great, Nadia thought irritably. *We have an audience.*

The killer, now identified as Lewis Fretz's embittered ex-wife, came at her again, stabbing at Nadia's abdomen. Years of martial arts training kicked in as Nadia deftly sidestepped the thrust. Stepping toward the other woman, she delivered an openhanded chop to Marlene's neck, striking her just above her left clavicle. The blow stunned the bogus tourist, giving Nadia a chance to grab on to the back of Marlene's neck with her right hand while simultaneously seizing the killer's knife hand by the wrist. She forced the blade away from her body.

"Wha—?" Marlene gasped in surprise. Despite her own training, she appeared to be rusty when it came to taking out an opponent who actually fought back. *Tough luck,* Nadia thought ferociously. She stepped backward to gain leverage over Marlene. *You're not attacking an unsuspecting actress or graphic designer this time.*

Exerting pressure on her adversary's neck and wrist, she started forcing Marlene to the concrete floor. Once there, she intended to pin the killer to the ground with her knees before disarming her once and for all. Marlene fought back, grunting fiercely, but her face slowly descended toward a cement impression of Jimmy Durante's nose. "Let go of the knife," Nadia ordered. "I'll break your wrist if I have to!"

She wasn't bluffing.

"Wow! This is great stuff!" An excited tourist ran out of the crowd, practically sticking his camcorder in Nadia's face. "Can you start over again from the beginning? I think I missed the first part!"

"Keep back!" she shouted at him. The alias killer had already proved her willingness to sacrifice innocent civilians; Nadia didn't want to give her a chance to turn this into a hostage situation. "Give me room!"

She struggled to hold on to Marlene, but the momentary distraction was all the other woman needed. Marlene viciously rammed her free hand into Nadia's stomach, causing the costumed agent to lose her breath, and then twisted free of Nadia's grip. She staggered across the cement tiles away from Nadia, with her fist still wrapped around the hilt of her knife. The crowd instinctively backed away, except for the idiot with the camcorder who seemed determined to capture the whole thing on film.

But Marlene wasn't interested in anyone except

"Abella." Knife in hand, she turned to confront Nadia from a couple of yards away. Murderous hatred blazed in her crazed hazel eyes.

"Who the hell are you?" she shouted at Nadia accusingly. "You're one of them, aren't you? One of those two-faced intelligence spooks who took advantage of my husband, then threw him away as soon as you needed a convenient fall guy!"

Close enough, Nadia thought. Recovering from the punch to her gut, she hurried to put herself between Marlene and the man with the camera. *I have to keep her focused on me, and not on any of these innocent people.* The crowd, however, still seemed to think this was all a show. More people poured into the forecourt, eager to find out what all the excitement was about.

"That's right, Marlene!" She used the woman's real name on purpose, to rattle her. Sneering contemptuously, Nadia unhooked her gold cape and waved it in front of her like a matador. "So what are you going to do about it?"

Fury twisted the killer's face into a grotesque mask. With a practiced move, she flipped the knife so that the tip of the blade was gripped between her fingers. "Take this, you CIA bitch!" she barked as she hurled the knife straight at the trademarked golden starburst emblazoned on the front of Nadia's costume. The quartz blade hit Quasar Queen's chest symbol dead on—and shattered against the armored plate underneath.

Good thing Marshall had reinforced Abella's cheaply made costume!

The crowd cheered and applauded at this live-action demonstration of the cartoon superheroine's legendary invulnerability, but Marlene was somewhat less thrilled at this unexpected turn of events. Her face fell as she grasped that she had disarmed herself to no avail. She turned and ran for the sidewalk beyond the courtyard. Her baseball cap tumbled off her head as she fled, revealing her sweaty and disheveled mousy brown hair. "Get out of my way!" she shrieked at the throng of tourists in her path. "Move, goddamnit!"

No way, Nadia thought. Marlene Fretz had already inflicted too much pain on the world—and Sydney. *You're not getting away again.* She hurled the golden cape like a net. Lead weights, sewn into the hem of the garment, carried it through the air before it dropped down on top of the fleeing murderer. The cape fell like a shroud over Marlene's head and she flailed about in confusion.

Nadia tackled her from behind. The two women crashed to the ground, and the crowd drew back in surprise. Marlene's body cushioned Nadia's fall, while the shimmering gold cape remained wrapped around the fugitive's head and shoulders. Rising up on her knees, Nadia took hold of Marlene's head with both hands, then smashed it against the cement, only inches away from Groucho Marx's handprints. The body beneath the cape went limp.

"Whoa there, tiger!" Weiss appeared behind her. He laid a gentle hand upon her shoulder. "We don't want to bash her brains out."

We don't? Nadia thought fiercely. *Even after all's she done?*

Still, Weiss had a point. There was something to be said for taking a prisoner alive. Taking a deep breath, she rose to her feet. She stood over her fallen foe as she assessed her partner. "Are you all right?" she asked.

"I may never eat another hot dog again," Weiss cracked, "but yeah, I'm fine." His greasy white apron clashed with the cold steel Beretta in his hand. "We need to get out of here before someone calls the cops."

Nadia knew what he meant. The less the CIA had to explain to the police, the better. She was glad that Marlene had not cursed Sydney's name in public. *We caught a break there.*

"Okay, everybody," Weiss said, raising his voice to address the gawking tourists gathered around them. "Show's over. Nothing more to see." Handing Nadia his gun, he squatted beside the cape-swaddled assassin and hefted her unconscious body from the ground. "Be sure to visit the gift shop next door."

A little girl stepped forward. Nadia recognized her as the same child who had asked her for her autograph earlier. The girl eyed Weiss suspiciously. "Who are you supposed to be?"

"Me? I'm Quasar Queen's boyfriend." He grinned at Nadia. "Aren't I lucky?"

INTERROGATION ROOM
APO BUNKER

Like the rest of the underground headquarters, the sleek white look of the interrogation room completely concealed the site's origins as an abandoned bomb shelter. White enamel walls contributed to the pristine, antiseptic ambience of the isolated chamber. Harsh fluorescent lights cast severe black shadows onto the tile floor. A one-way mirror allowed Sloane and a knot of agents to watch the proceedings unobserved. Closed-circuit TV cameras recorded everything that transpired, and soundproof tiles cut prisoners off from the rest of the world.

Just like SD-6, Michael Vaughn thought. He had never liked this room, although he conceded its necessity. Especially at times like this.

Marlene Fretz was strapped into a padded white dentist's chair. A canvas hood covered her head. Evidence extracted from her apartment was spread out on the clear glass table in front of her. She tugged impotently against her wrist restraints. Muffled profanities escaped the hood, which had been employed to conceal APO's location from her. Her carefree tourist garb looked distinctly out of place in the sterile interrogation chamber, with the Disneyland T-shirt striking a particularly discordant note.

"All right," Jack said coldly. He sat across the table from Marlene, his expression even more implacable than usual. "Let's get on with this."

Vaughn yanked the hood off Marlene. She

gasped eagerly at the fresh air. A swollen purple bruise covered most of her face; Vaughn barely recognized her as the same woman he had interviewed at the apartment building a few nights before. Damp brown hair was plastered to her skull and dried blood was caked around her nose and lips. *Weiss wasn't kidding when he said that Nadia had really knocked out Marlene,* Vaughn realized. He made a mental note never to piss off Sydney's sister.

"You!" Marlene blurted out, recognizing Jack and Vaughn. Her broken nose gave her raspy voice a congested quality. She glared at them with pure hatred. "I knew you two weren't really parole officers! The stink of the CIA was all over you."

The intensity of her anger came as no surprise to Vaughn. According to her military record, Cpl. Marlene Stafford (later Fretz) had received a dishonorable discharge from the U.S. Army after several disturbing incidents, including at least one instance in which she had physically attacked a superior officer. Her violent temper had cost Marlene her veteran's benefits and unemployment insurance, while severely curtailing her career prospects in the private sector. No wonder she had ended up at the 'Acienda Arms after her husband's career had gone down in flames as well.

Too bad we didn't look into her past sooner, Vaughn thought. *We might have seized on her as a prime suspect earlier.*

"So, what now?" she said venomously. "Are you going frame me, too? Just like you did Lewis?"

"We don't need to frame you, Ms. Fretz," Jack replied. He gestured toward the wealth of evidence lying on the table: a hit list; stalker photos; numerous disguises; a quartz knife, recovered from the forecourt of Mann's Chinese Theatre, that rested inside a protective plastic bag. "Don't try to deny it. We know you've committed at least five murders. The only question is whether you acted alone."

"Alone? Of course I was alone!" Saliva sprayed from her lips. "Who else did I have after Sydney Bristow and the rest of you betrayed my husband?" She nodded at the one-way mirror behind Jack. "Are you out there, watching this, Sydney? Don't you have the nerve to show your face?" She spit at the mirror. "You can't hide from me, bitch! Lewis told me all about you, about how you pretended to be on his side, year after year, before you finally double-crossed him!"

ALIAS

She squirmed violently in her chair, which had been prudently bolted to the floor. In similar straits, Sydney had once turned the tables on a hostile interrogator by flipping her chair onto her captor. Marlene had been deprived of that option.

"That will be enough," Jack said sternly. "For your information, Ms. Bristow is nowhere on the premises. As a matter of fact, she resigned from the CIA more than a year ago."

"Yeah, right," Marlene muttered, sounding unconvinced. "That still doesn't change what she did to us. For years Lewis served his country to the best of his abilities, but how did that lying slut repay him? She let him take the fall when you CIA slimeballs decided to pretend that you had nothing to do with SD-6. As far as I'm concerned, you all deserve to rot in hell."

Talk about deluded, Vaughn thought. Lewis Fretz could have come out of the SD-6 affair with his reputation intact, just like Dixon and Marshall had. Instead, he had made things worse by refusing to accept the truth and treating the CIA like the enemy. In the end his paranoia, and Marlene's anger management issues, had been a fatal combination for five innocent women. *What a waste.*

Jack didn't bother defending Sydney's actions. "We know that Lewis Fretz killed himself," he stated bluntly. "Did anyone else play a role in these murders? Does the name Oskar Murnau mean anything to you?"

"Who?" Marlene looked genuinely bewildered. "What are you talking about? Who's Oskar Murnau? Some other poor guy you're trying to smear?" Her fingers drummed restlessly against the arms of her chair. Vaughn guessed that she was probably craving a cigarette. "Well, you're not going to use me to ruin the life of another innocent man! Let Sydney Bristow do that. She's good at it!"

Vaughn had to speak up at this point. "Okay, we get it. You blame Sydney for your troubles. But what about Kate Jones and the others? Why did they have to die?"

"To make her face her guilt!" Marlene snarled. "To rub her face in the way her lies wreck the lives of ordinary people like me!" She strained at her bonds, throwing herself toward Vaughn and Jack. "I hope she thinks of those dead women every time she goes undercover to gain the trust of some poor sap she's planning to betray. I hope their deaths keep her up at night!"

Jack rose from his seat. He regarded Marlene as he would look at a particularly virulent bioweapon. He gathered up the evidence and placed it into a briefcase. "I think we've heard enough."

The older man's voice held not a trace of sympathy for the deranged woman, but Vaughn couldn't help feeling sorry for Marlene, despite everything she had done. Thanks to Lauren, he knew what it felt like to have your life turned upside down by a double agent. Had Lewis Fretz felt as betrayed by Sydney as he had by Lauren? Vaughn remembered the murderous rage that his wife's treachery had inspired in him. It was obvious that a very similar rage had driven Marlene Fretz insane. The tragedy was that she had turned that rage on the wrong targets.

She should have gone after Sloane instead.

Vaughn followed Jack out into the corridor, leaving Marlene alone with her thoughts of revenge. An armed guard was posted outside the door. Vaughn noted that Sloane was no longer present. Perhaps he had retired to his office to watch the interrogation.

"We'll want to subject her to a polygraph test

to be certain," Jack said, "but I feel confident that she acted alone. Apparently, Murnau played no part in the killings."

"So it seems," Vaughn agreed. He regarded Marlene through the one-way glass window. The captured killer struggled in vain to free herself from her restraints. "So what happens to her now?"

"In the old days, Sloane would have simply had her 'neutralized' permanently," Jack said, with perhaps a trace of nostalgia in his voice. "Now that we're under new management, I suspect that Director Chase will arrange to have Marlene committed to a mental institute secretly administered by the CIA."

Jack sounded as though he didn't particularly care where his daughter's tormentor ended up, as long as she never came near Sydney again.

Vaughn could hardly blame him.

Officially, he guessed, the alias killings would have to remain unsolved.

CHAPTER 13

LA PALMA
CANARY ISLANDS

"That's fantastic!"

Sydney was overjoyed by the news that the alias killer had been apprehended at last. She held her cell phone up against her ear as Dixon drove their rented jeep away from the airport. Vaughn's voice gave her a quick rundown on Marlene Fretz's capture and subsequent confession; it really sounded like the case had been closed for good. "Thank you so much, Vaughn. You can't imagine what a relief this is. Please tell Nadia and everyone else that I can't begin to thank them enough."

Vaughn said good-bye, and she took a moment to appreciate the people in her life. *I should have known I could count on them,* she thought. The spy business could be a dirty one, and she had encountered her fair share of deceit and betrayal over the years. At times like this, though, it was good to know that she also had friends and family who would come through for her when she couldn't do everything herself. *I'm not alone in this.*

"I haven't seen you smile like that for days," Dixon said. He steered the jeep south on C-832 toward the island's capital, Santa Cruz de La Palma. Steep volcanic slopes rose to their left, while the Atlantic Ocean crashed against the rocky seashore to their right. Lush green forests and plantations dotted the slopes before giving way to the barren summits of the Cumbre Vieja mountains. Sunshine poured down from a clear blue sky. "Good news?"

"Excellent news." She hastily brought him up to speed on the events that had transpired in Los Angeles. It was way past midnight there, she realized. She hoped that Vaughn and the others were getting some well-deserved rest.

"Poor Marlene," Dixon said, shaking his head.

"I met her a few times, back in the old days. She and Lewis had seemed very happy together." He glanced at Sydney. "So Murnau had nothing to do with the killings?"

Sydney shook her head. "Apparently not."

She rolled down the car window and inhaled the fragrant tropical air. It was a beautiful morning, made all the lovelier by the knowledge that no more of her namesakes would be killed. A great weight had been lifted from her shoulders—and her mind. No longer tormented by the senseless murders, she could finally give her full attention to Oskar Murnau and the missing Black Thorine, just as she should have done days before.

Time to get down to business.

She contemplated the gorgeous scenery. Sparkling streams flowed down from the mountains, and brightly colored flowers bloomed by the road. La Palma was also known as La Isla Bonita, she recalled. The Beautiful Island. Everything looked so idyllic and serene. What sort of agenda could Murnau possibly be pursuing here? According to his profile, Der Werwolf was fixated on the United States, which he blamed for the collapse of the Soviet empire—and the end to his glory days in the East German secret police. But La Palma's principal industries were agriculture and fishing, not tourism. American visitors were few and far between.

Except for Dixon and her, of course. Not wanting to be recognized by either Murnau or his people, they had made an effort to disguise themselves before exiting the plane. Mirrored sunglasses, a long blond wig, and a cowboy hat helped obscure Sydney's features. Tight jeans, a push-up bra, and a low-cut pink camisole had been deployed as weapons of distraction. The soles of her cowboy boots rested against the floor of the jeep.

"Let's hope we're as successful on our mission as our friends back home were on theirs," Dixon said. He had on mirrorshades of his own, along with false teeth, gray hair, and a garish Hawaiian shirt. A lightweight Panama hat protected his face from the glare—and suspicious eyes. "Any thoughts on where to start looking for Murnau?"

They were heading toward the capital by default, mainly because there didn't seem to be any other likely targets on the island. In theory, Der Werwolf had enough Black Thorine to blow the historic town off the map, but that still struck Sydney as pretty small potatoes for an ambitious terrorist like Murnau. *No offense to La Palma,* she thought, *but the average American couldn't even find this place on a map.*

"Beats me," she admitted. "Why go to all the trouble to manufacture an entire tank of Black Thorine just to stage a strike on a remote fishing community off the coast of Africa?"

A yawn escaped her lips. She hadn't gotten much sleep on the plane, and she could feel the long hours catching up with her. Her eyes burned, and her brain wasn't working as fast as she would have liked. She felt tired, worn out. *I'm running on fumes.*

"Maybe Murnau isn't after civilian casualties here," Dixon suggested. "Is there anything else special about this island?"

I wish I knew, Sydney thought. She rescued a self-heating can of coffee from the glove compartment and popped it open. Maybe a jolt of caffeine would sharpen her senses. She sipped the hot liquid as she mentally reviewed everything she had read about La Palma on the plane. What about the island interested Murnau?

La Palma's main claim to fame was the Roque

de los Muchachos Observatory, which boasted a massive telescope. High altitudes and the lack of big-city lights apparently made the island an ideal site for stargazing. *But so what?* Sydney thought. A major observatory still didn't strike her as a prime target for terrorism. Surely Murnau had not come all this way just to deliver a blow to modern astronomy. *That's not exactly going to throw America into a panic.*

Gazing out the windshield, her weary eyes took in the vast mountain range running down the center of the island. La Palma was not only the steepest island in the world, she recalled, but also the most volcanically active of the Canaries. The last major eruption had been a little more than thirty years ago. . . .

Her eyes widened. Was that it? "The volcanos," she blurted out. Inspiration and caffeine set her mind racing. "La Palma is one big chain of volcanos. That can't be a coincidence."

Gulping down the last of her coffee, she glanced at her watch. It was 10:15 A.M. here, which meant it was 2:15 A.M. in Los Angeles. *Sorry, Marshall,* she thought as she dialed his home phone number, *but the moon's coming up here in about nine hours. We can't afford to waste a single minute.*

It took a few rings to rouse Marshall, and Sydney was pretty sure she heard Carrie Bowman complaining in the background, but APO's resident genius eventually managed to stumble downstairs to his home office. Sydney put away her phone as Marshall set up a comm-link among Dixon, Marshall, and herself. A door clicked shut in Los Angeles.

"Okay," he said groggily. "What's up?" Sydney started to apologize again for waking him, but he cut her off. "Don't worry about it, really! I live for this stuff, you know that."

Sydney cut to the chase. "The volcanos, here on La Palma. What can Murnau do with a canister of Black Thorine and an island full of volcanos?" She had only the fuzziest idea of what to be afraid of—La Palma was still a long way from the U.S.—but she sensed that she was on the right track.

"Give me a sec," Marshall said. She heard him tapping at his keyboard, thousands of miles away. "Hang on! I think I've got something here. . . . Oh, no." His voice took on a hushed tone that instantly told Sydney they were in big trouble. "This is bad. This is seriously bad."

Sydney braced herself for the worst. "What is it?"

"There's a theory," Marshall began, "a fairly plausible one, actually, that the next big eruption on La Palma could send the western flank of the mountains sliding into the sea, triggering a mega-tsunami that could wipe out the East Coast of the United States."

"Dear Lord," Dixon whispered. "Is that truly possible?"

"You bet!" Marshall answered. "I'm reading about it right now. Back in 1949 an eruption caused the entire western side of the Cumbre Viejo ridge to slip several meters into the Atlantic. You can still see the fracture, which is about two miles long. Another big blowup could finish off the process . . . and send the whole thing crashing down into the ocean. We're talking half the island, some five hundred billion tons of land. That's enough to set off a tidal wave hundreds of feet high, moving at as much as five hundred miles an hour. At that rate, the waves would come smashing into the American coastline in ten to twelve hours, tops. Good-bye, Miami! Not to mention New York, Boston, Washington, D.C. . . ."

"We get the picture," Sydney said. A sudden certainty gripped her. "That has to be what Murnau is up to. He's going to use the Black Thorine to trigger an eruption and blast the mountainside into the sea."

Dixon shook his head. "But why go to such elaborate lengths? Why not just use the Black Thorine to attack America directly?"

"That wouldn't be nearly as cool," Marshall explained, "from a fiendish mastermind's point of view, that is. The damage you could inflict with just a high-powered explosive alone, while sure to be impressive, can't compare to the full impact of a major geological catastrophe. Disaster-wise, we're talking a whole different order of magnitude here." His voice didn't sound remotely sleepy anymore. "If you want the maximum bang for your buck, this is the way to do it."

"I'll take your word for it," Sydney said. Like the rest of the world, she had witnessed the widespread death and devastation wreaked by the 2004 Asian tsunami, as well as by Hurricane Katrina. Those horrific images made it all too easy for her to visualize what Marshall's megatsunami could do to America, and the world as she knew it. "Who knows? Maybe Murnau wants this attack to be mistaken for a natural disaster, or even the wrath of God."

Dixon nodded. "In any event, we have to stop this, no matter what it takes." He yanked hard on the wheel, executing a sudden left turn that sent the jeep speeding toward the looming volcanic ridge. Santa Cruz de La Palma, poised at the bottom of the slope, was no longer their destination. "Merlin, can you do a full, topographical analysis of the threat? We need to find out where exactly Murnau needs to set off the Black Thorine to achieve the desired effect."

"Right," Marshall responded. "I'm on it!"

"Copy that." Dixon's voice was grim. "Let us know when you have something."

The comms went silent as Marshall went to work. Dixon shared a worried look with Sydney. "I hope we're wrong about this," he said, "but I fear that's wishful thinking. This theory has Murnau written all over it."

That's what I'm afraid of, she thought.

Verdant fields of banana trees and tobacco plants rushed past them as the jeep headed inland. While Dixon kept his foot on the gas, Sydney consulted a map to get their bearings. The Cumbre Vieja ridge, the very spine of the island, stretched all the way to the southern tip of La Palma. "Head south," she advised him. If they wanted to get to the western side of the mountains, it might be easier to drive around the ridge than over it. Plus, that was where the more active volcanos were.

"Got it," he said, taking a right turn. They raced past sprawling green plantations while the sun crept higher in the sky. Dixon glanced up. "At least we have plenty of time before the full moon rises. If he sticks to his pattern, Der Werwolf will not set off the Black Thorine until nightfall."

"That's true," Sydney acknowledged.

Unless . . .

A horrible thought hit her. "Dixon! What if Murnau isn't timing his attack to nightfall here on La Palma, but on the moonrise back home?" La Palma was five hours ahead of eastern standard time, and Marshall had said that the tidal waves would take about twelve hours to reach America. . . . She frantically did the math in her head. "If Murnau wants the tsunami to hit the East Coast at around the same time the full moon comes up over Florida or DC, he needs to trigger the eruption sometime around noon,

La Palma time." She glanced at her wristwatch, which she had reset upon landing. "That's about an hour from now!"

Dixon didn't question her calculations. He sped up as he reestablished contact with Marshall. "Outrigger to Merlin, do you have that information yet? We need that location now."

"Hang on," Marshall responded instantly. He sounded like he hadn't budged from his computer. "I think I've got it narrowed down a little. You want Teneguía, the youngest and most active volcano. Its most recent eruption was in 1971. There are some fresh vents and cave entrances left over from that blast that would be ideal for Murnau's purposes, assuming that he's really planning to trigger La Palma's version of the Big One."

We can't dare assume otherwise, Sydney thought. She located Teneguía on her map. The volcano was at the southern tip of the island, not far from the small town of Fuencaliente. Dirt roads and hiking trails led up the mountain from the shore. She hoped there wasn't too much ground to cover. "Any vent in particular we should concentrate on?"

"Maybe one on the west side?" Marshall said

feebly. "I wish I could be more exact, but I'm still working on a precise location." Even over long-distance, you could tell how much he hated to disappoint them. "If you can get close enough, my Black Thorine detector might help you zero in on the explosive. I'm hoping it will be more accurate away from all that interference you ran into at the plant in Barcelona. I've also been fine-tuning the targeting software a bit. Let me uplink it to your unit right away."

"Sounds good, Merlin." Sydney retrieved the gamma ray scanner from the backpack at her feet, then hooked it up to her laptop. "Ready when you are."

The new and improved software appeared to download successfully. Sydney prayed that the detector would come through in the field this time. With time running short, they were going to need every break they could get. *Marshall knows what he's doing,* she reminded herself.

"Got it," she informed him over the comms. "Have you notified Sloane and my dad of the threat yet?" She knew the East Coast needed to prepare for the disaster, but she wondered if there was really any way to cope with a threat of this magnitude. Was it even possible to evacuate that many people?

"Done," Marshall assured her. "Sloane's yanking everybody out of bed. He's mobilizing the entire outfit. I think he's been in touch with Director Chase, too."

Sydney guessed that nobody in the U.S. intelligence community was getting much sleep tonight. She was grateful that her own loved ones were safe on the West Coast right now, a continent away from the ultimate target of the disaster. That would be small consolation, though, if millions of other people died in the catastrophe.

She looked at Dixon. His hands were gripped tightly around the steering wheel as he floored the jeep, racing down the back country roads toward Teneguía. Anxious furrows were etched deeply into his brow. Along with his dyed gray hair, the deep creases made him look much older than he actually was, as though Marshall's distressing news had prematurely aged him.

"Steven and Robin will be okay," she told him softly. She knew he worried about his kids at times like this. "California is a long way from the East Coast."

"I know." He smiled sadly at her to let her

know he appreciated her concern. "I just can't help thinking about all the other children, and their families, all along the East Coast." Sydney recalled that he had once lived in Massachusetts, while taking postgraduate courses at MIT. No doubt he still had friends and acquaintances out East. "They don't have a chance if that wave hits."

"We'll stop him, Dixon," she promised. "We have to."

It was nearly 11:00 A.M. by the time they reached the foothills of Teneguía. Blooming orchards and vineyards began to give way to semitropical wilderness. An arrow-shaped wooden sign pointed toward RUTA DE LOS VOLCANES. VOLCÁN TENEGUÍA. The Route of the Volcanos, Sydney knew, was a six-hour trail running the entire length of the Cumbre Vieja. Teneguía was the last or first stop on the hike, depending on where you started out. She pointed out the sign to Dixon, who turned left onto a dirt road heading up the mountain. The jeep bounced over the uneven terrain as Dixon pushed the vehicle to its limits while still maintaining control of the wheel. Sydney cradled the Black Thorine detector in her lap, trying to spare the sensitive instrument from the worst of the jolts. Her eyes anxiously tracked the sun's ascension; it struck her as perversely ironic that Der Werwolf would have to set off the eruption in broad daylight in order to strike America by the light of the full moon.

Some lycanthrope he's turned out to be.

They had driven less than a mile up the road before they met an obstacle. A heavy chain had been stretched across the road in front of them. An official-looking sign proclaimed in Spanish that a landslide had blocked off the road up ahead. Heavy block letters declared the way CERRADO.

CLOSED.

Dixon reluctantly slowed to a stop. He eyed the sign suspiciously. "Do we believe this?"

"You think Murnau or his people closed off the road?" At this point in their partnership, Sydney could read Dixon's mind sometimes. "To keep away any inconvenient sightseers?"

"That's what I would do," he said, "if I wanted to be undisturbed."

Sydney nodded. She swung open the car door and hopped out onto the ground. Drawing her Beretta from her purse, she approached one of the wooden posts holding up the chain. They had come too far to turn back now. "Let's find out," she said, squeezing the trigger.

A single shot shattered the links connecting the chain to the post. The rest of the chain dropped heavily onto the ground. Sydney grabbed one loose end and dragged it out of the way before clambering back into the jeep. She popped a fresh clip into her Beretta. "Road's clear."

Dixon hit the gas and they resumed their bumpy ride up the slope. Sydney was not too surprised when they failed to encounter any trace of a landslide, but the primitive roadway grew steeper and rougher every mile. A dense green forest, composed primarily of holly, myrtle, and laurel trees, hemmed in the road on both sides, but Syd was in no mood to appreciate the natural beauty of the woods. Visions of flooded cities and drowning families played across her imagination, reminding her of the terrible consequences of failure. She was accustomed to crisis situations, but the stakes today were even higher than usual. Thousands, maybe millions, of lives depended on her.

She glanced anxiously at her watch. The speeding jeep couldn't go fast enough.

"Heads up," Dixon warned her as they reached

the end of the road. A white and green four-wheel drive SUV was parked in front of them. A policeman wearing the dark green uniform of the Guardia Civil leaned against the driver's side door, smoking a cigar. Sydney recalled that tobacco was one of the island's major cash crops. *I'm running into enough smokers on this mission*, she thought. *If the terrorists don't get me, the secondhand smoke will.*

The jeep's arrival jolted the policeman into action. He took the cigar from his mouth and marched toward the jeep with a scowl on face. *"Cerrado!"* he yelled at them in Spanish. A holstered pistol rested against his hip. "The trail is closed. Turn back!"

Sydney and Dixon exchanged a look. Was this guy as authentic as that landslide warning a few miles back? Murnau had the resources to outfit a phony police officer, or even bribe the real thing. She stared past the guard at the slope beyond. A wooden marker indicated the trail up to the summit. One way or another, they had to get past this guy.

"Play this by ear?" she whispered to Dixon.

"My thoughts exactly."

Instead of turning the jeep around, they

opened their doors and waved at the policeman. Sydney tucked her Beretta securely into the back of her jeans, beneath the hem of her floaty pink shirt. Dixon hit the emergency brake but kept the engine running in case they needed to make a swift escape.

Smiling broadly, they stepped out of the jeep. Sydney hid the gamma ray scanner beneath the passenger seat, then made a big fuss of fumbling with her map as she exited the vehicle. *"Hola!"* she greeted the policeman enthusiastically. Her British accent was intended to allay the suspicions of any guards who might have been warned by Murnau to watch out for a young American woman. She hoped that the gunshot she had employed earlier to break the chain hadn't been audible here. "Do you speak English?"

"Buenos días!" Dixon added from the other side of the jeep. His accent matched Sydney's. He pulled out a disposable camera and started snapping photos of the startled policeman. "Smile!"

The guard reacted angrily. He snatched the camera from Dixon's hand, hurling it to the ground and crushing the fragile equipment beneath his heel. *"Váyase!"* he yelled at them. *Go away!*

Somebody doesn't want his photo taken, Sydney noted. That cinched it as far as she was concerned; this surly police officer was in cahoots with Murnau. *Good. That means I don't have to feel guilty when we deck this creep.*

She ignored his commands to leave. *"No comprendo,"* she said apologetically, politely overlooking his inhospitable behavior. *"Yo no hablo español."*

Growling, the policeman snuffed out his cigar on the hood of the jeep, then deposited the remains in his front pocket. His hand dropped onto the grip of his pistol. He gestured furiously at the road behind them. *"Váyase!"*

"Is this the way to Teneguía?" Sydney persisted. Her plan was to keep the guard occupied while Dixon quietly circled behind him. Fanning herself with the partially folded map, she leaned forward, offering him a generous view of her cleavage. "I hear the view from the summit is absolutely smashing!"

To her dismay, the man peered at her face instead of her breasts. His face took on a wary expression as he scrutinized her smiling features. Sydney had employed subtle makeup tricks to narrow her nose and enlarge her lips, but she feared that the rudimentary disguises weren't fooling Murnau's minions, especially if the goons had been specifically told to keep an eye out for a young white woman traveling with a middle-aged black man. She suddenly found herself pining for the latex wrinkles she had worn in Wilmington.

A blond wig and a British accent might not cut it here.

Peering over the guard's shoulder, she saw that Dixon was edging in toward the man from behind. She kept up a steady stream of chatter to keep the policeman distracted. "Do you remember when the volcano erupted last? That must have been terribly exciting!" A hint of anxiety entered her voice. She raised a hand to her lips. "There isn't any real danger here, is there? I mean, the volcano isn't going to blow up anytime soon, right?"

I sure hope not, she thought.

Ignoring her queries, the guard squinted at her sunglasses. *"Quite sus gafas!"* he barked, ordering her to remove her shades. When she feigned confusion, he reached out to pluck the glasses from her nose himself. His hand froze in midgrab, however, and his eyes suddenly widened in alarm. Sydney realized in horror that he had spotted Dixon

313

sneaking up on him in her mirrored lenses!

"Outrigger!" she called out to alert him, but the policeman had already yanked his gun from its holster. He turned to fire at Dixon, without so much as a word of warning. Sydney lunged for his arm, grabbing on to it with both hands and pulling it downward as the gun went off with a sharp report. Dixon cried out in pain.

No! she thought.

Clutching his leg, Dixon dropped to the ground. The policeman struggled to free his arm as Sydney fought to keep the gun pointed at the dirt. He punched her in the face with his left fist and Sydney saw red. She didn't care whether this guy was a real cop or not. He was going down hard. She gave his wrist a brutal twist and the pistol went flying from his fingers. Then, before he could react, she kicked his right leg out from under him, causing him to topple backward onto the ground. The back of his skull slammed against the earth. The impact left him stunned, but not unconscious, so Sydney finished him off with a vicious kick to his ribs, followed by a second kick to his jaw. His body sagged and his eyes closed.

Satisfied that the trigger-happy cop wouldn't

be getting up anytime soon, Sydney ran to Dixon's side. Her partner lay sprawled in the middle of the road, gritting his teeth against the pain of the gun-shot wound. Sydney saw that he had drawn his own handgun in self-defense. His Panama hat lay on the ground a few feet away. Blood pooled beneath his right leg, but she didn't see the jetting red spray of an arterial wound. It looked like the bullet had missed the major veins and arteries.

She dropped to her knees beside him. "How bad is it?" she asked.

"Could have been worse," he grunted with effort. Perspiration beaded upon his forehead and he spit the false teeth from his mouth. "Just a flesh wound, I think." He grimaced in pain, his whole body trembling. "Thanks for the save."

"I should have moved faster," she said regret-fully. Pulling a knife from her boot, she cut through his pant leg to inspect the wound. It looked nasty, but not immediately life threatening. The bullet appeared to have passed all the way through the fleshy part of his leg. "It was my damn sunglasses." She gently removed Dixon's shades so that she could see his eyes. "Stupid mirrors."

He shook his head. "He was onto us anyway.

315

But you can't worry about me now. I'll be fine."
Determination showed in his steady brown eyes.
"You have to complete the mission. Stop Murnau."
He gave her a pained smile. "I don't think I'm
going to be hiking up any volcanos today."

Sydney didn't waste time arguing with him.
He was right, of course. The mission took priority.
She hurriedly treated his injury with supplies from
the jeep, then tried to make him as comfortable
as she could in the few minutes she had to spare.
She propped him up in a sitting position against
the wheel of the jeep and made sure he had plenty
of water before she turned her attention to the
unconscious policeman. She bound the man's
hands and feet together with plastic cable ties and
locked him in the trunk of his own car as an extra
precaution. Recovering the man's gun from the dirt,
she thrust it into her belt for backup. No use letting
a good gun go to waste.

She checked her watch. 11:23 A.M. If Murnau
set off the bomb at noon, the resulting tidal wave
would engulf the East Coast around 7:00 P.M., just
in time for the full moon.

"I have to get moving," she told Dixon. She rescued the Black Thorine detector from the jeep and

put it in the small pack of supplies that was strapped to her back. To her relief, she could hear the siren of an emergency vehicle speeding up the road toward them. The ambulance would be here any minute. "You're going to be okay."

"Yes, I am," Dixon said. "Now do what you have to do."

The CIA was going to have to do some creative tap-dancing to keep this all quiet, especially if the guy in the trunk turned out to be a bona fide Spanish cop. But that was the least of her concerns at the moment. All that mattered now was stopping Murnau.

Without a backward glance, she sprinted up the trail leading to the summit. Soon she had left the dusty dirt road far behind. The winding path led upward through the lush vegetation. Her eyes searched the trail for the tracks of earlier hikers, but the rocky path offered no assurance that Murnau, or anyone else, had passed this way recently. She held the gamma ray scanner out before her like a divining rod. So far, its sensors had not detected any Black Thorine within its range. If Murnau was ahead of her, she still had a ways to go before she caught up with him. She came to a fork in the trail and turned left toward the western flank of Teneguía.

She hoped to God she was heading the right way.

It was a vigorous climb, and she quickly worked up a sweat. A few more hours of sleep would have helped, but years of physical conditioning had left her in good enough shape to tackle the hike even in a depleted state. Besides, this was hardly the first mountain she had scaled in her illustrious career. She sucked on a bottle of distilled water as she recalled climbing Mount Aconcagua in the Andes and Mount Subasio in Italy. Now, *those* had been tough.

The path grew steeper as she ascended. Sydney could see the foliage change with the elevation. Leafy ferns and laurels surrendered the higher ground to towering Canary pines, which somehow managed to set down roots despite the sharp angle of the slope. Sydney heard a mountain stream cascading somewhere in the wilderness, but she didn't have time to search for it. She reluctantly emptied the last of her water bottle.

The pines gradually gave way to the harsh, stony terrain of the *cumbre*. Only a few stubborn chrysanthemum bushes grew above the tree line, and Sydney swiftly left them behind as well. Reddish brown volcanic rocks dotted an almost lunar landscape, and hot air rose from patches of powdery white soil. The restless volcano rumbled beneath her feet.

Sydney was struck by the lack of any permanent monitoring station, despite the apocalyptic threat posed by the unstable volcanic ridge. *You'd think the rest of the world would want to keep an eye on this place.*

The trail became rockier and harder to navigate. Her backpack bounced against her shoulder blades, and loose gravel and scree slid beneath the soles of her boots. It was like trying to run over marbles. More than once, she slipped and had to break her fall with her free hand. Her left palm grew scraped and covered with powder, but somehow she managed to hold on to the gamma ray scanner with her right hand.

She was just starting to wonder whether the damn gadget was worth the effort when, unexpectedly, the handle of the detector thrummed against her palm, like a cell phone set on vibrate. Her heart pounded as she consulted the lighted display panel. The scanner was registering a sizable quantity of Black Thorine somewhere up ahead.

Murnau, she thought.

She didn't know whether to be thrilled or terrified. The good news was that she now knew for sure that she was closing in on him. The bad news was that the scanner's readings confirmed their worst fears about the German terrorist's ultimate objective. There was no longer any doubt in Sydney's mind. Der Werwolf was here to set off a disaster almost beyond comprehension.

Unless she could stop him.

CHAPTER 14

VOLCÁN TENEGUÍA
LA PALMA
CANARY ISLANDS

Marshall's improved software had done the trick. Working much better than it had outside Barcelona, the gamma ray scanner led Sydney straight to a rocky ledge on the western slope of the volcano. The ledge, which was about the size of a standard loading dock, looked out over the craggy coastline nearly twelve hundred feet below. Waves crashed against the sheer cliff face, and a fierce wind buffeted the exposed location, blowing her cowboy hat off. It went soaring out over the ocean. Looking north, she glimpsed the next volcano in the chain, San Antonio, only a few miles away.

There was no time to admire the view. It was almost noon. Murnau's window of opportunity had arrived, and he could trigger the eruption anytime now.

Sydney turned toward the granite slope that rose at the rear of the ledge. A vertical fissure, wide enough to step through, snaked its way up the side of the mountain. Hot air blew out of the crevice. Was this one of the volcanic vents created by the last eruption?

Sydney pointed the scanner at the jagged gap. The readings for Black Thorine were even stronger now. She was getting closer.

But would she catch up with Murnau before he could complete his obscene mission?

I have to, she thought.

Extracting a flashlight from her pack, Sydney took off her sunglasses and cautiously entered the fissure. The hot air blew against her face like the wind from a hair dryer. She kept the beam of the flashlight tightly focused on the floor right in front of her, for fear of alerting Murnau to her approach. The Black Thorine detector kept her pointed in the right direction.

The narrow fissure opened up to reveal a larger vent cut deeply into the granite shell of the volcano. Overlapping planes of hardened black lava coated the floor of the crevice. The air inside was uncomfortably warm and smelled faintly of sulfur. Despite the need for haste, Sydney had to tread carefully to avoid falling on the slippery obsidian path. Rounding a corner, she left the last of the sunlight behind. The granite walls were disturbingly warm to the touch.

She heard voices up ahead. Switching off her flashlight, she navigated by feel and sound alone until she glimpsed a bright white light farther down the passageway. She crept forward until she could make out the source of the light: an electric lantern being held aloft by the powerful arm of Greta, Murnau's pet Valkyrie.

Damn, Sydney thought. She should have known that the German's statuesque bodyguard would accompany him on this mission. *She probably hauled the Black Thorine all the way up the mountain herself.*

The two terrorists occupied a wide granite bridge spanning a seemingly bottomless chasm. Gusts of hot air and smoke billowed up from deep within the molten heart of Teneguía, along with a faint red glow. Greta provided the light while Murnau crouched in front of a familiar-looking steel canister. He seemed to be making the final adjustments to some sort of control panel mounted to the side of the metal tank. Their voices echoed off the igneous stone walls vaulting above them.

"Are you sure this is the right place, Oskar?" Greta asked. The female bodybuilder wore a sweat-soaked white tank top, khaki shorts, and hiking boots. Blond ringlets made her look like Heidi on steroids. An automatic pistol rested on her hip. "Maybe we should head deeper into the mountain?"

Murnau laughed harshly. "Trust me, *liebling*. You don't want to go too deep into an active volcano, not even a dormant one." Wearing a lightweight sport jacket and gray trousers, he consulted a handheld GPS unit. "No, this is the perfect location. Several brilliant geologists confirmed this before I dispatched them to their eternal reward. We have enough Black Thorine here to start a chain reaction that should split the entire Cumbre Vieja in half." He continued to fiddle with the control panel. "In just twelve hours, the United States—

that so-called superpower—will find out what a genuine force of nature feels like. We'll see just how arrogant the Americans are after their homeland is ravaged by a deluge of biblical proportions!"

Hiding in the shadows, Sydney felt her blood boil. Putting the gamma ray scanner aside, she drew her Beretta.

"What about the timer?" Greta asked. "Are you giving us enough to time to get away?"

"Have no fear," he assured her. "I'm setting the timer for forty-five minutes. The helicopter will be here to pick us up long before then."

Sydney wondered momentarily why Murnau hadn't simply taken a helicopter to the ledge in the first place. *I guess he didn't want to risk attracting too much attention before he had a chance to get the Black Thorine in place.* He must have known that his winery in Spain had not self-destructed as planned. Had he been worried about those maps of La Palma he had left behind? *Perhaps he was afraid that the CIA was waiting to shoot him out of the sky the first chance they got.*

"Let's get going, then," Greta urged him. Her boot tapped restlessly against the stone bridge. "This place feels like an oven!"

"Patience, my love," Murnau said. "I'm almost finished."

And then what? Sydney asked herself. She contemplated the gun in her hand. Did she dare fire the Beretta here within the volcano, where a stray shot or ricochet could set off the Black Thorine by mistake? She bit down on her lip in frustration. This was the winery in Spain all over again.

There was no point in trying to bluff with the gun. Greta would see through that in an instant. Sydney considered hiding until the murderous couple left, then trying to disarm the bomb before it went off. *That would be calling it pretty close,* she thought. If Murnau was to be believed, she would have less than forty-five minutes to stop the Black Thorine from detonating. What if she couldn't neutralize the explosive in time?

Putting her gun away, she drew out her knife instead. Eight inches of carbon steel protruded from the hilt. The direct approach was sounding better and better. If she moved quickly and quietly enough, she might be able to take them both by surprise—before Murnau had a chance to finish setting the timer.

It wasn't much of a plan, but it was the best she

could come up with on the spur of the moment. She quietly slid her pack from her shoulders and placed it securely against the wall of the passageway. *That's better,* she thought, stretching her muscles. She was going to need all the freedom of mobility she could get.

Keeping low, she crept furtively toward the two terrorists. Her fist was wrapped tightly around the hilt of her knife. *I need to take out Greta first,* she realized, *then Murnau.* Compared to his Amazonian bodyguard, the middle-aged spymaster would be a piece of cake. Or so she kept telling herself.

She made it halfway down the incline undetected, but irregular terrain and dim lighting got the better of her. The toe of her boot dislodged a heap of loose rocks, which clattered noisily down toward the bridge. Sydney winced at the racket.

The noise alerted her targets instantly. "What's that?" Greta exclaimed. She swung her lantern toward the sounds. The light exposed Sydney to her foes, throwing her shadow up against the rough granite walls. Murnau's face went from surprise to fury in an instant. "It's Sydney Bristow," he growled.

Greta's expression darkened. "You should have

died in Barcelona," she hissed at Sydney. She drew her gun from its holster. "I should have killed you myself!"

Was she willing to risk a shot so near the Black Thorine? Sydney didn't want to find out. Just as she had disarmed Kimber Grill in the garden, she hurled the weapon at the Valkyrie's wrist. The blade hit its target dead-on. Greta cried out in pain and anger as the knife cut her flesh. The Glock flew from her fingers, tumbling over the edge of the bridge into the volcanic chasm below. It disappeared into the smoking abyss.

The bodyguard plucked the knife from her wound. Only a few drops of blood dripped onto the granite bridge. Her eyes fixed like laser beams on the American intruder. "Don't worry about her," she instructed Murnau. "Finish up and get out of here." She smiled coldly; apparently, nothing took her mind off an impending apocalypse like a little old-fashioned violence. "I'll handle this bitch."

She set the lantern down beside Murnau, then charged toward Sydney.

Damn, Sydney thought. She didn't have time to go one-on-one with Greta right now. She raced down the incline, hoping to get to Murnau and the bomb, but Greta intercepted her before she could reach the bridge. The towering bodyguard planted herself squarely in Sydney's path. "Forget it," she taunted Sydney. "You're not getting any farther."

We'll see about that, Sydney thought. She sized up her opponent. Greta had several inches on her and was a bodybuilder to boot. Plus, she had Sydney's knife. *The only way I'm going to win this fight is by playing dirty.*

Fortunately, that wasn't a problem for her.

She feinted toward the right, then tried to dash past Greta on the left. But the huge blonde wasn't fooled by Sydney's ploy. Spinning toward Sydney, she slashed out at her with the knife. Sydney barely ducked beneath the blow in time. The steel blade sliced through the air above her head. Golden strands from her wig fluttered to the ground behind her.

Okay, that was close.

She yanked the policeman's gun from her belt, then used it to block Greta's next swipe with the knife. Sparks flew as the metal weapons glanced off each other.

Out of the corner of her eye, Sydney spotted Murnau racing past them toward the mouth of the fissure. The very thought of his escaping once more was almost more painful than any blow Greta could inflict, but she forced that out of her mind. *Never mind him,* she thought, *or Greta. I've got to get to that bomb!*

To fake Greta out, she backed up and swung the gun toward Murnau. "Don't go yet, Oskar!" she yelled. "I've still got a bullet for you!"

"No!" the loyal Valkyrie blurted out. Abandoning her attack for the moment, she threw herself between Sydney and her lover. For an instant Sydney could only wonder what inspired such fanatical loyalty in his bodyguards. Was it a shared hatred of America, or was Der Werwolf just a *really* great boyfriend?

I don't want to know, she thought. Instead of firing, she scooped up a handful of loose volcanic gravel, the same rubble that had betrayed her only minutes before, and hurled the rocky mix into Greta's face.

The Danish Amazon shrieked and clutched at her eyes. She slashed and grabbed blindly at Sydney, who dove under Greta's arms and somersaulted down the incline toward the bridge. Springing to her feet, she dashed for the bomb.

Please let there still be a chance I can disarm it, she begged.

She stumbled over a crack in the solid lava and hit her knee against a rock. The pain was excruciating, but she bit down on her lip and lurched to her feet. The delay had cost her precious seconds, however, and Greta had time to pounce on Sydney from behind.

Her powerful limbs caught Sydney in a bear hug, pinning Syd's arms to her side. "Forget the knife," Greta grunted in Syd's ear. "A witch like you deserves to burn." She lifted Sydney's feet from the ground and carried her, kicking and squirming, toward the bridge. Sydney could feel the scorching heat of the chasm rising up from below. "Nice wig, by the way," Greta muttered as she wrestled Sydney closer to the edge. The soles of Sydney's shoes dangled above the stone, unable to regain their footing. "This is for trying to steal my look!"

But Sydney gave as good as she got. Hooking her right leg around Greta's, she twisted around until they were almost face-to-face. Then she bit down hard on the Valkyrie's exposed neck, while simultaneously kneeing her in the groin. *What do you know?* she thought. *Blondes do have more fun.*

Screaming, Greta threw Sydney at the edge of the bridge. Sydney hit the ground hard and caught herself just before she rolled into the chasm. Greta glared down at her from only a few feet away. The bodyguard's eyes were red and irritated. Crimson teeth marks streaked her throat. "You dirty slut!"

Anger made the Amazon sloppy. She ran at Sydney to knock her over the edge, but Sydney rolled quickly onto her side and delivered a forward kick across Greta's legs. The startled bodybuilder tripped and flew headfirst off the bridge. A shrill scream trailed off as she plummeted into the magma far below.

That's two of Murnau's girlfriends I've taken out now.

Sydney had neither the time nor the inclination to mourn Greta's death. Looking around for Murnau, she saw that the master terrorist had indeed fled the vicinity. She swore under her breath, but kept track of her priorities. Der Werwolf could wait. The bomb was what mattered right now. Thank God the electric lantern had survived the fracas.

Scrambling to her feet, she rushed over to the deadly steel canister. Glowing green numerals ticked down on the control panel, which Sydney guessed was the firing mechanism as well. Her heart sank as she read the display on the timer:

00:04:37.

The bomb was set to go off in less than five minutes!

"No!" Sydney gasped. Had Murnau lost his mind? That wasn't nearly enough time for him to get away from the catastrophe he was about to set into motion. Was he willing to die just to get his revenge on the United States? Apparently so. She recalled how Sloane had described Murnau back in the briefing room at APO. *"A true fanatic."* Sloane had been right.

"Phoenix to Merlin," she paged Marshall. She was going to need serious technical assistance if she was going to defuse this bomb in four minutes. Her fingers cautiously probed the black steel casing of the firing device. It appeared to be welded shut. "Merlin, please respond!"

Nothing but static came over the comms.

I'm too far inside the volcano, she guessed. The dense granite walls were blocking the transmission.

She was on her own.

"Damn!" Now what was she supposed to do?

She didn't have a bomb disruptor, not that it mattered. According to Marshall, Black Thorine was considerably more volatile than plain old C-4. After a bit of waffling, he had decided he simply couldn't guarantee that a high-pressure water burst wouldn't set off the superexplosive.

An awful realization came over Sydney: She wasn't going to be able to disarm the bomb.

That left her with only one alternative. She had to get the bomb as far away from here as possible.

Grunting, she hefted the thirty-pound tank into her arms. Murnau had said this spot inside the volcano was the ideal place to set off the Black Thorine if you wanted to kick-start a megatsunami. Sydney prayed that he knew what he was talking about.

She raced up the slippery lava passageway, clutching the heavy steel canister against her chest. The viscous black fluid sloshed sluggishly within the tank, and the blinking green numerals flashed beneath her face.

00:03:31.

Daylight beckoned ahead of her, filtering through the fissure at the top of the passage. Sydney remembered her cowboy hat flying out over the Atlantic. If she hurled the canister off the cliff, would that be far enough from the vent to keep the inevitable explosion from tearing the Cumbre Vieja apart?

It's worth a shot.

She ran toward the light, a hot wind at her back. Her battered bones and muscles ached from the brawl with Greta, but that didn't slow her down. She sprinted through the fissure and out onto the rocky ledge outside. The sudden glare of the sunlight compared to the murky depths of the volcanic vent caused her blinking eyes to fill with tears, but she raced toward the edge of the cliff . . . only to be struck brutally from behind by someone lurking just outside the fissure. A hard, steel object slammed into the back of her head.

"Where is Greta?" Murnau demanded furiously. His fist was wrapped around the barrel of a Glock automatic pistol. "What have you done with her?"

Sydney staggered forward, dazed by the blow. Her thick blond wig had provided a degree of protection, but her skull still hurt like hell. She could feel a massive goose egg already beginning to form.

Her hands still full of Black Thorine, she turned to confront her ambusher. "Sorry, Siegfried," she taunted him. "You're going to need another Brunhild . . . again."

Homicidal fury contorted his face. His freakish yellow eyes bulged from their sockets, and his clenched teeth flashed beneath his drooping mustache as spittle foamed at the corners of his mouth. His gray-streaked black hair was wild and disorderly. Not even a real werewolf could have looked so maniacal.

"I'll kill you, you bitch!'

Sydney was barely listening. The countdown on the timer consumed her attention.

00:02:25.

The edge of the cliff was only a few yards away. She stumbled toward the brink, holding on to the metal tank with all her strength. But Murnau was too fast for her. He darted between her and the precipice, his Glock aimed at her face.

"Not another step!" he snarled.

Sydney heard the waves crashing below. She was so close!

"Don't be insane!" she pleaded, in a last-ditch attempt to reason with him. "You're going to get us both killed!"

"I don't care! Just so long as America feels my wrath!" His entire body quivered with suicidal mania, but he kept his pistol pointed at Sydney.

"You Americans think the fall of the Berlin Wall was so inspiring!" He spit onto the rocks at her feet. "We'll see what you think about the fall of your precious American empire!"

His eyes zeroed on the timer beneath her chin. A flicker of anxiety showed upon his bristling face, as though he was afraid that the Black Thorine was already too far from the volcano's interior to achieve the effect he desired. "Back into the vent!" he demanded. "Now!"

Forget it, Sydney thought. *That's not going to happen.*

Holding the metal tank up in front of her, she charged at Murnau. He fired wildly, the bullet chipping a chunk of granite from the mountain behind her. She swung the heavy canister toward her enemy. "You wanted this damn stuff so much? Take it!"

The canister slammed into Murnau like a battering ram, knocking him over the brink. His arms flailed about frantically as both he and the Black Thorine plummeted out of sight. His scream sounded eerily like the howl of a dying wolf.

Sydney had let go of the canister at the moment of impact, but her momentum had carried her over the edge as well. Gravity seized her, and she reached out desperately for the ledge. Five fingers snagged onto a granite outcropping jutting out from the rocky shelf. She swung face-first into the sheer cliff, but she succeeded in grabbing on to the brink with her other hand too.

She couldn't see her watch from her present position, but she closed her eyes and counted down the seconds.

The explosion sounded like the end of the world. A tremendous plume of seawater sprayed upward from twelve hundred feet below, drenching Sydney and nearly shaking her from her precarious hold on the ledge. Her fingers ached as they supported the entire weight of her soaked clothes and body. She held her breath as she waited to see if Oskar Murnau's nightmarish doomsday scenario had survived him. Had the Black Thorine brought about Oskar's deluge?

The rocky face of the volcano shuddered against her. Fragments of stone rained down on her, pelting her head and shoulders.

But the Cumbre Vieja held together. There would be no tsunami today.

Exhausted, her ears ringing, Sydney dragged herself back up onto the ledge.

Mission accomplished.

LOS ANGELES

"Welcome home!" Nadia greeted Sydney as she returned to her own house, no longer threatened by the alias killer. "Here, let me help you with your bags."

"Thanks," Sydney said. She paused in the foyer to savor the familiar sights and smells of home. Her dad's safe house had been comfortable enough, but there was no place like home. "Did I miss anything?"

Nadia carried Sydney's suitcases into the living room. "Eric called. He and Vaughn are coming over

339

later with pizza and DVDs. I figured that would be okay with you."

"Sounds perfect," she said. She made a mental note to invite Dixon and his family over sometime soon. His leg was healing nicely, but he probably wouldn't mind a little help looking after his kids for an afternoon. She was tempted to extend the same offer to Marshall, but the "terrible twos" sounded almost more intimidating than the Covenant and K-Directorate combined. *Maybe we'll hold off on that invitation until Mitchell is a little older.*

"Oh, one more thing," Nadia added. Sydney heard a trace of apprehension in her voice. "Eric is picking out the movies. He says he's got something special, just for me." Her face took on a deadly serious expression. "Please tell me I'm allowed to kill him if he brings over any 'Quasar Queen' cartoons."

Sydney laughed. "I'll have to check the Agency protocols and get back to you." She sank down into her favorite easy chair. Her tired eyes gazed wistfully around the room.

Nadia sat down on the couch. "Seriously, how are you doing? You've had a rough couple of weeks."

"Seriously?" Sydney appreciated Nadia's concern. "I'm happy to be home, and even happier that the alias killings are finally over." She shook her head sadly. "What happened to Lewis and Marlene Fretz is awful. I know I did the right thing taking down SD-6, but I never considered the effect it would have on people's real lives."

Nadia laid a comforting hand on Sydney's leg. "You saved infinitely more lives by bringing down SD-6 and the Alliance. And by stopping Murnau from setting off that tsunami. In the long run, you've done way more good than harm. Unlike, say, Murnau."

"You've got a point there." Sydney felt her spirits lift.

She remembered her last glimpse of Der Werwolf as he plunged into the sea below Teneguía, taking the lethal Black Thorine with him. The fact that no tombstone marked Murnau's watery grave struck her as grimly fitting. Whereas she had far too many namesakes, Oskar Murnau had taken his own name with him to his death.

I can live with that, she thought.

Greg Cox is the *New York Times* bestselling author of two previous Alias novels, *Two of a Kind?* and *The Road Not Taken*. He also wrote the official novelizations of *Daredevil*, *Underworld*, and *Underworld: Evolution*, as well as numerous books and stories based on such popular series as *Batman*, *Buffy the Vampire Slayer*, *Fantastic Four*, *Farscape*, *Iron Man*, *Roswell*, *Star Trek*, *X-Men*, and *Xena: Warrior Princess*. His official website is www.gregcox-author.com.

He lives in Oxford, Pennsylvania.